THE TRICKLE OF TIME

THE TRICKLE OF TIME

By Anne Jobes

PEN PUBLISHING

Jobes, Anne, 2010
        The Trickle of Time, First Edition, November 2010;
Second Edition, April 2014
Includes historical references.
ISBN 144994096X (soft cover), EAN-13 is 9781449940966,,
Book # 3415273

    1.   Slavery, Underground Railroad, The Emancipation
          Proclamation, historical fiction

LIBRARY OF CONGRESS CATALOGING-IN-
PUBLICATION DATA

I would like to thank Jessica Winberg for her honest approach
in reviewing and assisting in editing the contents of this book.

Hope is the thing with feathers
that perches in the soul
And sings the tune without the words
And never stops at all.

-Emily Dickenson

Preface

"Thus have I been attacked at midnight with fire and weapons of death, and nothing but the good providence of God has preserved my property from flames and myself and family from violence and death. And why? Have I wronged any one? No, but I am an ABOLITIONIST. I do not recognize the slaveholder's right to the flesh and blood and souls of men and women. For this I must be proscribed, my property burnt, and my life put in jeopardy! Now I desire all men to know that I am not to be deterred from what I believe to be my duty by fire and sword. I also wish all to know that I feel it my duty to defend my HOME to the very uttermost, and that it is as much as duty to shoot the midnight assassin in his attacks as it is to pray."

-Reverend John Rankin, Ripley, Ohio 1841

Introduction

Henry and I had known one another all our lives. His family belonged to the MacDonald's who owned the plantation runnin' on the southernmost corner o' our land. Henry was the eldest o' five children, and the only boy.

I was 'bout a year younger than Henry. His mama had passed on when Annabelle (his youngest sister) was born. But before that, my mama and his would chat every chance they'd git, and us youngin's would tag along.

Henry and I'd spent hours in the summer sunshine playin' in the fields when we wasn't doin' our chores. Sometimes we'd even visit with one another in one o' the little sheds our families lived in.

Henry's papa, Jacob, didn't like me much. I don't suppose it was me he didn't like – it was that when I was around, Henry sorta lost track o' time, so Henry's papa thought I was nuthin' but trouble. He always had to remind Henry to git to workin', and sent me off home.

Henry told me that he usually got the switch too, but he didn't mind none. We was fast friends, Henry and I, and I think we'da gone through jus' 'bout anything for one another.

It was natural, I guess then, that Henry'd be the one to bury me, and care for my sister with his own life.

But I guess I'm gittin' ahead o' myself.

Maybe I should start at the beginning...

Chapter One

On a warm September morning in 1842 a young black southern slave named Isabelle gave birth to a son. Her midwife cleaned the child in warmed corn oil, wrapped him in a blanket of soft cotton, and handed him to his mother to nurse. Her husband, Isaac worked the fields all day. He came home long after the sun had set, curled up in the bed with his wife and new child and fell immediately to sleep.

Isabelle and Isaac were plantation slaves that had been purchased by Tom MacDonald. Master MacDonald was a wealthy land-owner and one of the most successful farmers in Kingston, Alabama.

Isabelle and Isaac were two of the twenty-four slaves acquired in Hickory Grove, Montgomery County five years before. They met for the first time on a hot July afternoon. Being chained together for the long, rough trip to Kingston, both feeling frightened and unsure, they shared a kinship that blossomed into romance 18 months later. Not long afterwards, Isabelle and Isaac were married in a small, ramshackle chapel and together began to make a life for themselves as they served the family who owned them and their kin.

Master MacDonald, like any other slave owner in the Deep South was nothing more than a terrorist when it came to the treatment of his slaves. Even the most kindly and humane of masters knew that the threat of violence was the only power that would force the gangs of field hands to work from morning until night like an army that wouldn't question what needed done or solicit better treatment. It was common to have recurrent public floggings to remind slaves that there was a heavy price to pay for unproductive labor, rebellious behavior or refusal to accept the Master as greater than them.

In this world of abuse, disrespect and demeaning cruelty, Henry's parents found deep solace in their faith, their community and in the love they had for one another. Back-breaking work could not absolve who they were.

Two and a half years after they were married Isabelle realized that she was with child. The joy she felt was tempered with concern about her baby's future welfare, the thrill of new life and the hope it inspired created a feeling of deeper commitment to her husband, and a sense of normalcy in her world.

The pregnancy was uneventful and when her time came, she called a midwife from their small community on the plantation to help her through the process. For Master MacDonald this was another slave to eventually work his land. To the community of slaves that were known as the MacDonald Negro's however, this baby was a black American born child and the celebration each person felt was very personal. It was a new beginning and a reason to hope that someday, perhaps in this child's lifetime, all slaves would be free to own their own land and farm it the way they desired. There were already rumors of a conflict on the horizon as many slaves had escaped to the north where some were already permitted to live free.

In Alabama, slaves were fed, clothed, housed and provided medical care in the most minimal manner. In many households, treatment of slaves varied with the slave's skin color. Darker-skinned slaves worked in the fields, while lighter-skinned house servants had comparatively better clothing, food and housing. As masters applied their stamp to the domestic life of the slave quarter, slaves struggled to maintain the integrity of their families. Slaveholders had no legal obligation to respect the sanctity of the slave's marriage bed, and slave women—married or single — had no formal protection against their owner's sexual advances. Without legal protection and subject to the master's whim, the slave family was always at risk.

Isabelle knew several of the women had been raped by Master MacDonald. With the birth of her first child (although the possibility was very real that he could be beaten when he was grown), she was still glad for a boy so that she might avoid the pain of watching her daughter become one of the Master's distractions.

As time went on, more children were born to the slaves at the MacDonald plantation. Isabelle and Isaac were blessed with three girls by the time Henry was nine years old. The little quarters where the MacDonald slaves lived had become a small village, and although they were mistreated, they were strong in their feelings of kinship and leaned heavily on their faith to find peace in their existence. Master MacDonald allowed them Sunday off, and for that they felt deeply blessed. It was a day of worship, fellowship and family gathering.

It was also a day for Henry to sneak off and visit with Delia.

Chapter Two

My Daddy died when I was 'bout twelve years old. He got the fever and nuthin' my Mama did could stop his passin'. I remember Mama cryin' all the time that first year after he died, and I took to watchin' my sister and brother for her, keepin' 'em outa trouble, and makin' sure they did their chores.

I missed my Daddy a lot but there weren't no time for grievin'. I was the one to clean the rooms, do the laundry and make sure the kids collected the eggs and fed the livestock. Mama spent all her time in the kitchen, watchin' Master's youngin's and doin' the mendin'. We was happy to work in the house and Daddy always used to say that we should count our blessings – so we always did.

It was jus' after Daddy passed that Master Hayes took me to his bed the first time. I didn't know what he was doin' - I jus' did as I was told.

He told me to meet him in his bed chamber. I thought I was goin' to git beat for not doin' somethin' right. Mama looked worried, but I told her I'd be fine.

When we got to his room, he closed and locked the door. I was kinda scared causin' he'd never locked the door before. He walked over to me and hit me real hard across the face. I fell down but I didn't yell out. Papa always said that if ya yelled out they had more power

over ya. So I kept quiet, but I remember my
eyes filled with tears.

Master told me to take off my clothes. I
weren't sho' why but I knew not to question
him. I was so scared. I took them off kinda
slow. In my mind I kept thinkin' that I might
be allowed to stop. Maybe he was jus' testin'
me or somethin'. But the whole time I was
undressin' Master had a real frightenin' look on
his face. I noticed his brow was shiny from
little beads o' sweat that had gathered there.

Once my clothes was off I remember wishin'
I could jus' hide somewhere – wishin' he'd jus'
leave. But that weren't the case. He was
lookin' down at my twelve-year-old body
without really lookin', ya know? He pushed me
toward the bed, told me to git on top o' it, and
then he started to take off his clothes too.

I knew enough from livin' on a farm what
happens when two folks git together like this. I
jus' didn't know why Master was doin' this with
me. He didn't give me much chance to
consider it neither. He slapped my face again,
and then again. He forced my legs open and
pushed himself into me so hard that it felt like I
was tearin'. I screamed, and this time he
punched me. I felt the world go dark, and for a
few minutes I weren't feelin' nuthin'.

I don't know how long until he dismounted
me, but when he did, he put on his clothes
again and told me to wash the comforter on the

16

bed – told me to be sho' there weren't no stains, and he left the room.

I sat up. Everything hurt. I looked down and saw a lot o' blood – my blood. My lips was bleedin' too. I had to move real slow causin' it hurt so much, but I got myself dressed, stripped the bed, and went to wash the comforter.

Master raped me several times a month after that. But it weren't never as bad as the first time – that is, until the very last time.

Chapter Three

As I grew up I spent more and more time with Henry. We'd find all sorts o' excuses to git out o' the house and meet up somewhere. 'Course there was times when things didn't work out but we was pretty lucky – especially on Sunday afternoons after church services. There was always a little time in between church n' supper preparations where Henry and I would walk by the river and talk.

By the time I was 'bout fourteen and Henry was fifteen, we was talkin' every week after church. My Mama knew where I was and who I was with. She liked Henry and in the back o' her mind I know she was fixin' to see us hitched some day. She knew what Master did to me and I think she was hopin' that if'n I was to move off to Master MacDonald's plantation I might be spared.

Henry and I was always prim and proper. We didn't hold hands or nuthin' until we was older. At fourteen I was still pretty naïve. Even though Master was doin' that awful thing to me all the time, it was like I was jus' doin' my duty – a chore – and after a while it weren't nuthin' personal.

But Henry – well, he *was* personal. He was my best friend in the world. We shared all sorts o' things with one another – things that had gone on during the week, stuff within our families – what we liked and didn't like – and even our most private thoughts. At that point I hadn't shared what Master was doin' with me all the time. I jus' knew – even though I didn't take it none too personal – Henry would be upset. In fact, he'd be downright mad. Since there weren't nuthin' he could do anyway, I didn't think it was important to talk 'bout it with him.

"Delia," Henry started, as we walked along the river. "Jus' wonderin' – did ya ever think 'bout what it'd be like to be free? I mean, not livin' under somebody else's rules – 'cept God's, o' course."

"Sho', Henry," I replied. "Lots o' times. I jus' cain't quite picture it clear though. I mean, how'd we know what to do next? We has the rules o' the house that we follows all the time. How'd we live without them rules?"

I really had no vision at the time o' freedom. THIS was freedom to me: walkin' by the river, talkin' with Henry. Even in the winter when the winds blew cold we'd find a warmer spot, build a little fire and talk for hours.

"I don't know if'n I'd like freedom too much, Henry," I stated honestly. "If'n we was free then we wouldn't be livin' where we's livin' now and ya and I wouldn't be taken none o' these walks on Sunday's like we does now." I looked at him and smiled. "I don't think I'd like that none."

Henry stopped and put his hand on my shoulder. "Now, Delia. Ya know I wouldn't let

19

nuthin' like that happen. Heck, I'd marry ya if'n I had to! You and I jus' gotta always be able to take these walks." He smiled his devilish smile, and as he started to run a bit on the path yelled back to me, "If not, I couldn't beat ya in no more races!" And he laughed as he gave me little room to catch up.

By the time we got to the swimmin' hole we was both laughin' and out o' breath. Since we was in our Sunday best, and we was gittin' older now, we didn't strip down to swim no more. But I always took off my shoes and stockin's and waded into the warm water. Henry rolled his pants up, and talkin' off his shoes and socks too, he strolled in beside me. The water felt real good. August in Alabama kin be swelterin' and I almost wished I could lay back in it and float downstream.

"There's talk, Delia, 'bout blacks that live in the north livin' free lives. They're livin' in their own houses and workin' their own jobs. There ain't no Master – jus' them," Henry said. "If'n I could go north, Delia, I would. Would ya go, I mean, if'n ya could? Would ya be scared to go?"

I thought 'bout it for a minute. I don't suppose I'd ever thought 'bout living free in that way. I guess I figured if'n we was freed then we wouldn't have no where's to live.

"Well, if'n there was a way to have a house and a job, Henry, and if'n I could care for my own youngin's then, sho', I might be goin', if'n I could."

I don't suppose I thought it'd be possible to do such a thing really, and I wondered if Henry had heard wrong. Still, it was kinda a nice thought, and Henry and I both walked slowly in the water parallel with the shoreline in our own silence considerin' it.

Chapter Four

By the summer o' 1860 my baby brother
Josiah and my younger sister Winnie were five
and seven years old. I was nearly seventeen
and bein' a house slave, I was in charge o'
makin' sho' the youngin's did what they was
supposed to do. There weren't no schoolin' for
none o' us, so our days was spent cleanin',
pickin' weeds, and makin' sho' the chicken's
was fed. Even though they was young, they
learned easy and they did what they was told.

Mamma was always cookin' and cleanin' in
the kitchen. She picked the fresh vegetables,
canned 'em for winter, and did a lot o' the
growin' too. She served the food, went to the
market (I got to help her with that sometimes)
and cleaned up everything nice n' shiny after
each meal.

In the wintertime there was fireplaces to be
set and cleaned, beds to be warmed, and wood
to be chopped. There were men folk who did
some o' the heavy work – mostly they was field
hands. The overseer who was in charge used
every man, woman and child to make sho' the
tasks that needed to be done was completed
quickly. Sometimes he was scarier than
Master. When he got to whoppin' it was like he
couldn't stop. I was always scared o' him and
kept the little ones out o' his way.

It was that summer, one Sunday mornin'
after church services that Henry told me he had
to talk to me straight away. He seemed real

serious and I weren't sho' if everything was okay. We walked kinda quick like and real quiet. Finally, when we got to the river, Henry asked me if'n I had heard 'bout the fightin' that was goin' on.

"I ain't heard nuthin', Henry." I paused. "Who's fighin'? What are ya talkin' 'bout?"

"Delia," Henry took my hands. He was lookin' at me so serious like, it kinda scared me. "There's lotsa colored folks who's free. There's places up north where people don't think we should be treated like animals – that we should be treated like people. Delia, I'm wantin' to go those places. I want to be free. I want to have a payin' job and buy me a house, git married, and have youngin's. I don't wanna work for no slave master who don't do nuthin' but make money offa my hard work."

Henry's voice sounded strong – like he had some kinda mission or somethin', but I didn't understand what he was sayin'.

"Henry, why ya tellin' me this? Ya leavin'? Are ya goin' somewhere's without me?" I felt really worried.

He looked at me. His eyes softened. He put his hand on the side o' my face. "Naw, Delia. I ain't never goin' no where without ya." He took my hand and we started walkin' down the path.

"I think we should git married, Delia. Maybe next year. I'll wait for ya. Then we kin both leave and go north." He stopped and put his hands on my shoulders. "Will ya go with me?"

I cain't say what I was feelin' jus' then. It was like I jus' couldn't see my life without Henry in it, but I didn't have nuthin' to picture 'bout goin' somewhere's else neither. I mean, what would we do? How'd we live? Would someone jus' give Henry a job? I had no idea what it even meant to go north. Heck, I didn't even know where north was.

"Henry, I been hopin' for a long time that you and I'd git married someday. I mean, I cain't think o' no one but you bein' my husband, but why cain't we jus' stay here? We got us a place to live and work to do. We got our kin."

We sat on a big rock that looked out over the water. Henry seemed like he was far away – seein' somethin' I didn't. "Delia," he said, kinda sad like. "I don't wanna leave my family but I'm willin' to go without them if'n they don't wanna try to git away from this Hell we was born into." He turned to look at me straight away. I looked into his eyes. They were familiar to me. Almost like lookin' in a mirror sometimes. But this time I wasn't quite sho' what he was thinkin' or feelin' and it was peculiar to me. "If'n I go, Delia, will ya go with me? I'll wait 'til you's ready but we gotta make plans. We gotta decide."

I looked at him. He meant so much to me that I couldn't picture my life without him. I looked out to the river. It seemed so peaceful but I felt kinda torn apart. I loved my Mama, my brother and sister. I had cousins and friends that I cared for. Was he askin' me to leave everyone? Was he askin' me to choose between him and them?

Finally, I spoke. "Henry, would ya go without me?"

He breathed real deep like. "I don't want to, Delia. I cain't imagine life without ya in it. But I cain't stay here forever. If'n ya don't wanna go – I'm gonna have to go without ya."

I felt like he had smacked me in the face. I looked at him. I didn't understand. It was like he was sayin' that he didn't care 'bout me. "You'd leave me?" Tears stung my eyes.

"Oh, Delia," he said as he took my hand in his. "I don't know how I'd ever go without ya, and I'm hopin' I don't have to. It's jus', when I hear tell o' colored folks livin' like whites – their kids not gittin'' beat 'cause they missed an egg in the hen house, it makes me think 'bout my own youngin's and what I want for them. I know they ain't born yet, but that don't make me want any less for them, ya know?" He looked at me. "I wants more for you and me too, Delia. I want us to live free lives." He was quiet for a minute. Then he looked away from me. "I knows what yer Master does to ya. He does it to all the women-folk. They all do." He looked back at me again, and put his hands upon my shoulders. "I don't want that for my own daughter. Do you?"

I looked down. I hadn't never thought o' it like that before. It hadn't never occurred to me that one day my baby might go through what I was goin' through. It wasn't right. I knew it wasn't right. I even had to worry 'bout Winnie. I hadn't thought none 'bout that neither – 'til jus' then.

"Henry," I said as I looked at him. "I'll go with ya. I'll go with ya when ya goes up north. But I wants to take Winnie - and Josiah too. I cain't have them here if'n I ain't here to protect them. Promise me we kin take them with us, and I'll go anywhere's ya wants me to go."

Henry smiled. "We'll take them, Delia." He laughed and pulled me into a light hug. "We'll take them too!"

Chapter Five

In November o' that year we got ourselves a new president. Normally we wouldn't care much 'bout that (it weren't usually gonna affect us none), but there was talk that Mr. Lincoln wanted to free all the slaves and so we was all excited and wonderin' what that'd mean to us if'n he was able to do that. We knew there was a war brewin', and though that was kinda scary, we was glad people was fightin' to help us have our own lives.

Even though Mr. Lincoln built a reputation o' bein' against slavery, most o' the south made it known that this was going to split the United States up. In December, jus' before Christmas, a separation happened that *did* divide the country. First, South Carolina left the union. After that, Alabama, Florida, Georgia, Louisiana and Mississippi did the same thing. Before we knew it, there was tell that we weren't a part o' the same country no more – that we had started our own country called the Confederate States o' America. Pretty soon other states joined us and a civil war was on verge o' takin' place.

From the beginning, both colored folk and free men saw this as a chance to help break the chains o' slavery. Some slaves decided to stay with their masters and even decided to fight against Mr. Lincoln's army. Henry'd git so mad when he heard 'bout that 'cause he said it was kinda like fightin' against his own brothers and sisters.

"Delia," Henry said to me after church services in the spring o' 1861, "I'm thinkin' I ought to help with the fight. There's talk o' a Negro army that's formin' and I kin join 'em."

"Henry, you ain't joinin' no army! You could git yerself killed! I know ya care 'bout all this, and I'll go with ya anywhere's but I ain't havin' ya dead somewhere's jus' to prove some point!" I was angry. I was scared. "You gots to promise me, Henry, that ya won't go fightin' in no army." I was almost cryin'.

"I'll promise ya one thing, Delia. I won't go fight less'n I haveta, but if'n the time comes that there ain't no good reason not to, I'm gonna join that army if'n they'll have me. I'll fight for yer freedom even if I gotta die doin' it!"

I loved Henry's passion but as the months passed, the more we heard 'bout the fightin' that *was* goin' on, the more frightened I became.

It was late spring, nearly summer, when Master put on a grey uniform and went off every day to meetin's. We didn't know where he was goin', exactly, but we knew he was tryin' to keep us slaves as his property. Sometimes he'd be gone for longer than a day but I didn't git the idea that he was actually fightin' himself; he jus' sorta seemed to be plannin' somethin'.

I always liked when Master was gone.
Sometimes me and Henry'd meet in the trees
way out in front o' the house in the middle of
the afternoon. I wasn't allowed to ever be in
the front o' the house. Mama'd git real mad at
me if'n she found out I'd been out there. Henry
and I didn't pay much mind to that, though.
We wanted to see each other more often than
jus' Sundays.

Master's house was a big whitewashed brick
house. It had big white shutters on the
windows and big white pillars on the veranda.
There was six wide steps that went up to the
porch and beautiful flower gardens that
encircled the pathway where people'd come up
to the house in their fine carriages. Gardenin'
was done only in the early mornin' and only by
one slave named John who had lived in our
quarters longer 'n any other coloreds Master
owned. If'n John saw me 'n Henry he'd have
probably tol' the overseer that we was out front
so we was always careful not to meet 'til we
knew ol' John was workin' in the back.

One real warm spring afternoon I met Henry
out front. The sky that day was real blue and a
nice breeze was blowin'. When I got to the
place where Henry was meetin' me, he was
already standin' there with a big mallet in his
hand. He was dressed in a blue shirt and a pair
o' pants that was real old and tore, but he was
the handsomest man I'd ever seen.

"What are ya doin' with that, Henry?" I
asked smilin'.

"I come over from mendin' fences when I seen the sun so high in the sky. I knew you'd be here soon, but I cain't be here long, Delia. I got to git back before they miss me." He smiled at me.

Where we stood was all surrounded by trees. If'n we moved further out toward the house we could see it, but from where we was no one could see us, and we wasn't able to see them neither. It was like a secret world that only belonged to me and Henry.

"Sometimes I wish we had more time together. We's always havin' to sneak around and then in a few minutes we always has to be done," I said.

"Well, I'd make an honest woman outa ya, Delia. If'n ya marry me, we kin see each other every day." When Henry talked it was like everythin' was always okay.

"There ain't nuthin' in the world I'd rather do, Henry." I reached out and took his hands. I knew it was a bold move – especially since we was not bein' chaperoned but Henry and I'd known one another forever, and there weren't nuthin' wrong with holdin' his hands. I knew there weren't.

"You sayin' 'yes" to me, Delia? You gonna marry me, then?" Henry smiled real big – almost like a child – and I giggled. I knew I was gonna marry him. There weren't nobody else I'd ever love like I loved Henry.

30

"O' course I'm gonna marry ya, Henry. You already know that."

He looked at me, kinda happy – kinda serious like. "When, Delia? When is we gonna git hitched?" He bent down on one knee and smiled real big. "You need me to ask ya all proper like?" He put his right hand on his heart, and held my right hand with his left one. "Delia, will ya marry me?"

I laughed but then I looked at him, and I wondered why we wasn't married already. "Yes, Henry. I'll marry ya."

He stood up, put his hands around my waist and picked me up. "Yee haaa!" He spun me around and I laughed and laughed. When he put me down he hugged me real tight and said, "You jus' made me the happiest damn slave in the south!"

"Henry, ya gotta stop whoopin' and hollerin' – we's gonna git caught out here. Who knows where old John is." But I was smilin' too.

"I gots to go, Delia. I gots to git back to my work but I ain't gonna sleep at all tonight – I'm so excited! You start plannin' a weddin', okay? We'll git married before the leaves starts to fall."

"Okay, Henry," I said with a smile. He touched my face with his hand.

"I love ya, Delia"

"Me too, Henry"

And with that, he walked back toward the MacDonald land. I stood there watchin' him walk away. I felt so happy that day. I wrapped my arms around my own body and closin' my eyes; I turned my face up toward the sky, and sighed.

All o' a sudden', though, I had a feelin' like I was bein' watched. I looked around, listenin' for any sound that wasn't supposed to be there. I held my breath.

Nuthin'. I jus' must'a been out here too long.

I started walkin' back toward the house.

Chapter Six

As I broke through the tree-line at the edge o' the big grassy yard in front o' Master's house, I saw his carriage sittin' there. The horse was hitched to the post. That'd mean Master had come home and somehow me and Henry hadn't heard him. I jus' had to git back into the house without him seein' me.

I runned across the yard as fast as I could and bounded up the steps real quick. As slow as possible I opened the front door and peeked inside. I didn't see no one. I didn't hear nuthin'. I closed the door behind me, and as I passed the sittin' room on the left and the study on the right, I glanced into both rooms. No one was there.

There was a big, wide staircase right in the entryway and beyond it was the doorway to the kitchen. I peeked up the stairs as I made my way to the kitchen. Nuthin'.

When I walked through the doorway I seen Mama standin' by the sink. She looked at me with a worried look on her face but she didn't say nuthin'. I took a couple o' steps toward her. "Mama," I began, but the look on her face tol' me Master was standin' behind me.

My heart practically stopped beatin'. I closed my eyes. *"Please don't let him be there,"* I thought.

When I turned around I saw Master standin' there with an angry scowl on his face. Master was a very large man. He had a full, grey beard and icy blue eyes that were raging. I knew I couldn't say nuthin' to him. I knew I was gittin' beat.

"Outside!" he bellowed pointing to the kitchen door. Mama jus' looked at me. She couldn't stop him. There wasn't nuthin' she could do.

I went outside. I was scared. "I's sorry, Master. I won't never do it again," I said tryin' to convince him that I'd obey from now on.

"To the barn!" he screamed.

The barn was way across the back yard. I kinda ran to it, knowin' I was in big trouble, not knowin' how bad I was gittin'' beat, but knowin' I couldn't do nuthin' 'bout it. I opened the door. It was dark inside.

As soon as I went in I turned around. The back o' his hand hit my face before I even saw him there. I fell to the dirty wood floor. My face was stingin' but I didn't have no time to think 'bout that. Master pulled me up by my hair and hit me again. This time I fell toward one o' the empty stalls. There was soiled straw on the floor but I was glad for it 'cause it softened the fall a bit.

I opened my eyes and as I rolled over I saw Master takin' off his belt. "This'll teach you not to heed my rules!" And he started hittin' me with the belt. Each time the leather touched my body my skin burned like it was bein' lit on fire. Once or twice I felt the buckle strike my body or my head, and it hurt so much I wasn't sho' I'd see the light o' day again.

I was cryin' – screamin' – but he kept up. All curled into a ball on the straw I couldn't even open my eyes no more. Then he started kickin' me. He was bellowin' on and on 'bout me bein' a stupid nigger and I'd do what *he* wanted me to do 'or else.'

Somewhere in the background I thought I heard Mama screamin' and callin' for Henry to come but it seemed like a dream to me. I was too hurt to know what was real.

Then Master started to rape me. He tore my britches off, forced my legs apart and shoved himself into me so hard that it felt like a knife cuttin' me inside. All I could do was cry and hope he'd stop and go away.

When he was done, he pulled himself outa me and with his heavy boot he kicked me again before he walked away.

As soon as he was gone I heard the sound o' my Mama's footsteps. She came around the corner o' the stall and screamed. She called for Josiah to run and git Henry. She held me in her arms and rocked me. Everything in my body hurt. I tasted blood in my mouth. I knew my face was swolled up 'cause I couldn't hardly open my eyes. My head felt like it was 'bout to explode. But it was my stomach that hurt worse. Somethin' weren't right. I felt like I was dyin'.

I looked up at Mama. She had tears in her eyes. "Oh, Lord," she was sayin'. "What'd he do to ya? What'd he do to my baby girl?"

Jus' then Henry was beside me. The look on his face was full o' fear. I knew I must'a looked real bad. But in that moment I also knew that I weren't gonna make it neither. I really was gonna die and there's weren't nuthin' Henry or Mama could do.

I tried to speak but I was chokin' in my own blood. Mama wiped my face with her apron. I felt her tears spill onto my arm.

"Delia," Henry said to me. But he didn't know what else to say. He had tears too.

"Henry," I whispered. He bent down to hear me. "Don't let him do this to Winnie." I took another slow breath. "Take care o' Winnie..." I took one more breath and then I passed on.

Chapter Seven

I don't remember nuthin' for a long time after that; it's like everything went dark and my mind weren't workin' no more. But I do remember the day they buried me under the big ol' tree by the outbuildin's.

I felt like I was floatin' a few feet off the ground, and lookin' down onto my wake. Everythin' seemed like there was some kinda blue filter coverin' over it. The day was dark. It had been rainin'. There was Mama, Josiah, Winnie and Henry standin' by the hole they'd dug up to put me into. Lots o' other folks was standin' close by too but it was like I could only clearly see my family – and Henry too, o'course.

My body was wrapped in a white sheet and tied with rope around the neck, waist and ankles to keep the sheet in place. There weren't no wooden box or nuthin'. Our preacher man was standin' beside the graveside and was sayin' a prayer. I couldn't hear what he's sayin' but Mama was cryin' real hard. Henry had his arm around her and the kids was standin' on the other side. They looked more scared than sad to me.

I don't know how long it lasted 'cause I didn't have no sense o' time at all, but after a while everybody started headin' back toward the house 'ceptin' a couple o' men folk who shoveled dirt down onto what used to be my body. Henry walked back with Mama and then

I don't remember nuthin' else for a long time after that.

Chapter Eight

Henry's mind was numb with sadness and ablaze with anger. He was well aware that there wasn't anything he could do to the man who had killed Delia. As soon as he'd walked her Mama back to the house, he needed to get back to his chores. He'd patted the kids on their heads and promised all three of them that everything would be fine.

Walking through the yard to the property line all he wanted was revenge. The preacher man had gone back down to the ramshackle church to put away his Bible before he got back to his chores as well. If he hadn't, Henry would have gone and talked to him. He knew that the rage he felt wasn't a Christian feeling.

He decided that the only way to handle what he was feeling was to run. As his feet picked up speed, he began to feel more and more irate. The angrier he felt, the faster he ran. As he ran across the soft fields of newly planted tobacco there was a deep pain that began rising up in his chest. The anger was turning into a feeling of deep grief and he began to feel sick to his stomach.

He slowed down and began to gag. Panting heavily, his eyes blurred with tears. Henry heaved until there wasn't anything left inside. He fell to his knees and began crying. The tears exploded more ferociously than the vomit he had just thrown up. In his mind, he saw Delia's face – her smile – and he felt an emptiness he could never have imagined before. His heart was broken. How could she be gone? He couldn't envision not talking with her – walking with her – hearing her laugh again.

He blamed himself. Why hadn't he heard the carriage return? Why hadn't he been able to protect her?

With his face in his hands, he sobbed until there were no tears left. He shook his head and screamed, "Why?" to the heavens. Kneeling in the quiet tobacco fields, his body weak from sorrow he began to feel the silence around him. In that moment, it was as if he could hear her voice one last time, *"Don't let him do this to Winnie. Take care o' Winnie..."*

And suddenly, he knew exactly what he had to do.

Chapter Nine

The following Sunday after church services were over – when he and Delia would have normally been spending time together – Henry stayed long after all the other people were gone, and talked with the preacher man about escaping to the north. He asked him what he'd heard, and if he knew what could be done to get out of the south before all Hell broke loose and they were in even more danger than that which every day life offered them now.

At first the preacher seemed fearful of the discussion but he'd known Henry all his life and knew real determination when he saw it. If he didn't help the boy, no doubt he'd find someone who would. Besides, he figured it was mostly grief speaking and that after a certain amount of time passed, Henry would just forget these wild dreams. In the end, the preacher agreed to find out what he could. When Henry left the churchyard that day, he was certain that it would only be short time until he and Delia's family were free.

Weeks went by without any word from the preacher. Every Sunday when service was over and everyone was shaking the preacher's hand, Henry'd give him a questioning look but the preacher man would only shake his head "no" and look away. Henry was as patient as he could be. He knew it wasn't something that could easily happen overnight. He didn't even really understand what it was that actually going to happen. He just knew that he had to get out and he had to keep Delia's Master from hurting Winnie.

Every few days he'd visit briefly with Mama and check to see if she was doing okay. He'd ask about the kids and he'd visit Delia's grave.

One late Saturday evening, when he was supposed to be asleep, he left his blanket-swathed, hay bed and crept quietly out of the house. He moved through the night easily. The moon was high in the night sky and the stars were shining like diamonds on a velvet bedspread. Within ten minutes he had arrived at Delia's graveside. It had been nearly two months since she had been killed. Her grave lay peacefully under a soaring willow tree. In the soft summer night air, Henry could smell the sweet fragrance of roses from the formal gardens in the front of Master's house. He knelt down putting his hand upon the mound of dirt that covered Delia's body, and closed his eyes.

"Delia," Henry said to her. "I misses ya so much. I jus' wish I could talk to ya again." He paused, opened his eyes and looked up to the sky. "I know you's out there somewhere's, Delia. I knows you kin hear me. I jus' want ya to know, I's goin' git yer family outa here. I's making plans. Preacher man's helpin'. I won't let nuthin' happen to Winnie, Delia. I promises ya. I'd do anything for ya, Delia." Reaching over, touching the earth one more time he said, "Anythin.'"

Chapter Ten

The next thing I remember seein' was Henry's hand tryin' to somehow touch me through the dirt. I was standin' beside the makeshift cross Mama had placed at the head o' my grave. Henry had tears in his eyes but I didn't really feel bad. I knew everythin' was gonna be okay. Henry didn't – but he'd find out. We was gonna see each other again. I knew we was.

Listenin' to Henry talk to me, I jus' knew I had to talk back. I waited 'til he was quiet. He was jus' sittin' there lookin' straight ahead, kinda starin' but not lookin' at anythin' particular.

I squatted down in front o' him. *"Henry,"* I said. *"It's me...Delia. Kin ya hear me, Henry?"*

He didn't seem to take notice o' what I'd said. Instead, he hung his head kinda low and sighed real big.

I reached over and touched him on the head. *"Henry, I'm right here."* I paused. *"Cain't ya hear me, Henry?"*

He lifted his head and looked around. I thought, *"Maybe he hears me!"* and I was real excited like. I knew that if'n I could git through to him, he'd feel lots better.

This time I got real close and looked right in his face. *"Henry...listen...I'm talkin' to ya. Kin ya hear me at all?"*

Henry paused. Again, he looked around. "Delia, if'n I didn't know no better, I'd swear you's talkin' to me." He shook his head. "But that's silly, ain't it? You's up in heaven." He looked to the sky. "I know ya is, cause there ain't no where's else you'd be able to be."

I weren't frustrated or nuthin' 'cause I knew I'd git him to hearin' me somehow or other.

"Delia, I wish ya knew how much I misses ya." He seemed lonely. "I miss talkin' to ya, Delia. I miss walkin' by the river with ya. I walks there every Sunday anyways. It makes me kinda sad but happy too, ya know?"

He hung his head. I reached over again, and touched it. I leaned in real close again, and touching his arm too, I said as clear as I could, *"I'm fine, Henry. You don't need to be sad."*

Henry lifted his head. He looked around as if he'd heard somethin'. He leaned forward and looked around the tree he was sitting beside as if he's gonna see someone on the other side o' it. Finally, he said, "Delia, you're out there, ain't ya?" He paused. I smiled. "I know ya is. If'n you kin hear me, Delia, then I want ya to hear real clear – I'm gonna come back here tomorra too, and we'll talk more. I'll talk to ya every night 'til I leaves here. I loves ya, Delia."

He stood up. With a small smile on his face
he sighed, and walked on home.

"I loves ya too, Henry."

Chapter Eleven

For many years before Master killed me there was people up north workin' hard to try to give black folks a chance for freedom. Jus' like Henry'd tol' me, there was folks who believed that America could be filled up with people who was different colors and they'd all have equal rights. The people who believed like that called themselves, abolitionists, and they wanted to do away with slavery all together.

They put forward this definition o' a 'Birthright Citizenship': "*Anybody born in America is a citizen, black or white, doesn't matter. And they are citizens of the nation, not just of the state, and are entitled to the same equal rights as all other citizens of the nation.*"

These men and women was made up o' both white and black, rich and poor, politically minded or o' revolutionary mentality. They all had one common hope: that men and women o' all color should be free.

Because they believed in this right, they created a movement that was supposed to help colored folks run away to the north so's they could be liberated. There was already lots o' Negros up north that had enjoyed bein' free for years. They still worked for white men, o' course, but they got paid a day's salary for a day's pay. They went home to their homes and families at night, jus' like everyone else. Some black folks even started their own businesses in the north.

But in the south things was different. Most
men believed that black people were jus'
possessions. Although lots o' masters was
good to their slaves and gave them their
freedom after so many years, many more o'
them was cruel and unjust. The abolitionists
believed that no man should be treated like an
animal.

Lots o' the men folk in the quarters where
my family lived, and all around the county, had
meetin's where they talked 'bout how they
needed to git away. These meetin's had been
goin' on for quite a while and though they's
usually only for the older men folk, the
preacher man finally tol' Henry where the
meetin's was bein' held. So Henry got to
listenin' in. Sometimes he'd cross property
lines to find out what was goin' on. Sometimes
he'd git caught away from where he was
supposed to be, but he didn't care none. He
was fixin' to go north. Lotsa black folks had
already escaped from Alabama and Henry
weren't goin' t' wait no longer.

There was talk o' a way to git away – that
there's people who'd help. There was a whole
other language they was using – like a code
that people'd know who could help them
escape, and who would not. Some o' the
people they called "Sheppard's" was livin' in
Birmingham, jus' outside o' Kingston where
Master MacDonald and Master Hayes
plantations was. These agents would be able to

help the coloreds who wanted to run away, git away.

There was a whole mess o' folks helpin' people to escape the prison they's born into. Henry found out that there was hidin' places along the way that whites was helpin' blacks stay so's they weren't caught while they was tryin' to flee.   Lotsa free black folks was helpin' too, o' course, and Henry started makin' his plans.

Henry would come by my graveside every night for months and tell me what he'd found out and how he was gonna help Mama, Winnie and Josiah. Sometimes when I'd talk back to him, he'd act like he's hearin' me. Other times it'd be like I's screamin' at him and he couldn't hear nuthin'. It was always nice, though, to see him sittin' there, talkin' to me. I liked listen' to his voice.

One night in mid-summer he tol' me that he was fixin' to leave soon. He'd been talkin' to lots o' people who could help him know where to go and how to know how to git help. He said he was ready. He tol' me he was gonna talk to Mama tomorra.

"Delia, there's a mess o' people who kin help us and with a war startin' I don't want to wait no more. We don't know what's gonna happen if'n we end up breakin' free from the country for good. I don't wanna see my children's beat and raped by selfish white men who don't see nuthin' but the color o' our skin."

I smiled. Henry had such a great heart.

"Henry, I'll be there tomorra with Mama when ya tells her. I'll help, if I kin."

I reached over and put my hand inside his. After a couple o' minutes, Henry looked down at his hand. He was holdin' it real still – like he didn't wanna move it.

"I swear, Delia, I know it's probably all in my head, but sometimes it seems like you's right here with me – holdin' my hand and all."

"I is, Henry. I'll always be right here."

Chapter Twelve

Mama was out in the garden pickin' parsley when Henry approached her. "Hey, Mama, how ya doin' today?" Henry asked.

"I's fine, Henry. How ya doin'?" Mama kept pickin'.

Henry looked around. "Mama, I gots to talk to ya 'bout somethin' that's real important."

"Well, go ahead an' talk, boy. I gots work to do so if'n you's gonna talk, ya gots to help me pick while ya talk," Mama said to him with a smile on her face.

Henry bent over and started pickin' parsley and puttin' it in Mama's basket.

"Mama, ya know anything 'bout the Underground Railroad?"

"The what?" she asked, still pickin'.

Henry looked around again. "There's people helpin' slaves to escape, Mama. They's a bunch o' 'em. There's people they call "Conductors" who helps people git to the next place, and people who helps the slaves hide. They's signs that people puts out on trees and stuff so people knows where to go. They call it the Underground Railroad. Ain't ya never heard o' it?"

"I heard o' it, boy. " Mama stopped pickin'

and looked at Henry. "Why ya talkin' 'bout this, Henry? Boy, you ain't got no crazy ideas rollin' around that head o' yers, do ya?"

Henry kept pickin'.

"Mama, I's goin'. I ain't stayin' here no more. I ain't raisin' no youngin's under some slave Master's whip! Folks has been leavin' for years an' lots o' 'em is free now – livin' lives like human bein's instead o' dogs."

Mama seemed a little angry. "Henry, I always thought ya was a smart boy. I wished Delia and you'd o' had a chance to git married. But jus' as many people's dyin' out there as is gittin' freed. Folks is gittin" caught and brought back and beat so bad they cain't see straight. Why'd ya put yerself through that when pretty soon we'll be freed anyway?" Mama started pickin' again. "That new President's gonna fix things. You wait an' see."

"Mama," Henry started, "Mama – look at me a second." He put his hand on her arm. She looked at him.

"Mama, I'd like to think the fightin's gonna help us but we don't know for sho'. What if it don't work? I ain't waitin' around. I heard 'bout a place called "Ripley" in the state o' Ohio. All we has to do is cross the river and we's free. There's a man by the name o' Rankin – I think he's a preacher man or somethin' – and he's helpin' slaves find their way to freedom."

Mama looked at Henry with doubt in her eyes. "Henry, there ain't nuthin' I'd rather do than be free. We don't know nuthin' else, for sho', but I'd figure it out if'n I had to. But, boy, where do ya think 'north' is? How ya gonna git there? You gonna walk? I been hearin' 'bout black folks gittin'' shot tryin' to escape. Yer Master MacDonald would rather shoot ya than have ya runnin' free. Why don't ya jus' wait it out – see what happens?"

"Mama, I don't want to be arguin' with ya 'bout this. I'm goin' and no one's gonna stop me." Henry stood up. Mama looked up at him. "I's jus' tellin' ya, Mama, 'cause I's fixin' to take Winnie and Josiah with me. I wants ya to come too but if'n ya don't, I have to take them youngin's away from this. I promised Delia that I'd take care o' Winnie – not let what happened to Delia happen to Winnie – and I won't, Mama – even if I have to protect her with my own life."

Mama's eyes got real big. She struggled to stand quickly. She wasn't old but years of hard work and firm beatings had taken their toll on her body.

Henry's hand went out to steady her. She got up close to Henry's face. "Look here, boy, I loves ya like a son but you ain't takin' my babies out o' here, riskin' their lives for *yer* dreams. At least here they's safe. I don't like bein' no slave any more than you do. I really hopin' Mr. Lincoln's war helps us." She

52

paused. "I was there when Delia asked ya to take care o' Winnie – not to let these things happen to her. But what if'n somethin' happens to them while you's out runnin' in the woods? How would I live with myself if'n I didn't know they was safe?"

"Mama," Henry said, "they ain't safe now."

She looked into his strong eyes. "You think on it a bit, Mama. I's leavin' soon."

And Henry walked away.

Chapter Thirteen

There was lots o' times when I didn't have no awareness o' the things that was happenin' on our plantation. There was times when I weren't able to talk to Henry or even hear him. I don't know why such a thing happened but it didn't bother me none. I always knew everythin' was okay so I jus' did what I did, when I did it.

I won't never forget the day that Henry took Winnie and left for the north.

I felt like I was floatin' near the ceiling o' the kitchen – the same kitchen where Master forced me outside jus' before he killed me.

Mama was there, in front o' the sink. She was cryin'. Henry was standing in front o' her with a satchel o' Winnie's things. Josiah and Winnie were standing next to one another lookin' kinda scared, a little sad and mostly confused.

"Mama," Henry was sayin', "I promise I'll take good care o' Winnie. You don't never need to worry 'bout that."

"I knows ya will, Henry. And I knows you're right 'bout her goin'. After the way Master was yellin' at her yesterday, I knew ya was right. It wouldn't be long before he'd be hurtin' her like he did my Delia."

"I'll take Josiah too, Mama – and you. We

could all go." Henry reached over and put his hand on Josiah's head.

"I'd jus' slow ya down, Henry. I cain't have ya gittin'" caught for the likes o' me. And ya cain't take two youngin's. It's hard enough to make this kind o' trip with one."

Mama knelt down. "Come here, child," she said to Winnie.

Winnie ran over to Mama and wrapped her arms around her. "Mama, where's I goin'? Ain't ya comin' too?" She had big tears in her eyes.

I knew Mama and Winnie's hearts was breakin', but I knew, too, that Henry had to git her out o' there.

I watched the scene, and I felt sad for them, but real proud o' Henry at the same time.

"Say goodbye to yer brother, Winnie," Mama said. "You'll be seein' him again real soon. Henry'll come back an' git us all once this war is done."

Josiah was only five years ol' so he didn't know nuthin' 'bout what was happenin'. The kids hugged one another. Henry took Winnie's hand and with one last look, Henry took Winnie out into the darkness.

I stayed jus' a minute after they left. Mama knelt down and told Josiah that he wasn't to tell anyone 'bout Henry takin' Winnie no matter what.

"Okay, Mama. I won't tell," he said.

And that's all I remember for a real long time.

Chapter Fourteen

There were a lot of slaves in the mid-1800's who had fled the bondage of their confinement. To slave masters or sympathizers of the south these slaves almost seemed to magically disappear under the cover of darkness. Although many slaves were hunted down and found, countless others were able to escape without a trace. Slave Masters and others began to say that they must be getting away on an "underground (invisible to the eye) railroad," and that's where the Underground Railroad got its name.

This escape network was really an underground resistance movement. The system used secret meanings that were shared in code words, hand signals, as lyrics in songs and markings on trees or fence posts. By word of mouth, slaves and abolitionists were able to tell escaping slaves where safe houses or meeting places might be. There were small, independent groups of people that maintained secrecy but knew very little of any other "stations" other than the ones they were connected with. Escaped slaves would move along the route from one way station to the next, steadily making their way north. "Conductors" on the railroad came from various backgrounds and included free-born blacks, white abolitionists, and former slaves.

The first part of Henry's escape was saturated with difficulty. The routes for the underground railroad mostly moved from Kentucky and northward or Texas and southward. Alabama had no real distinct routes in place. Henry knew that if he were lost and not sure which direction to take that he should travel at night and follow the north star. No matter where he was, the north star would guide him.

He also knew that he would have to deal with hunger, slave masters that might have dogs sniffing them out and the responsibility of a frightened little girl who might often cry herself to sleep.

For the first few nights Henry traveled shorter distances. He followed the night sky, hiding under the canopy of trees that lined cotton fields and rows of tobacco. Sometimes he had to carry Winnie over rough brush. Other times she was so brave it was almost as if she were carrying him.

Winnie learned to be quiet – to talk in whispers – and to be patient.

On the fourth night, as they made their way over a slight hill they spied a beautiful sight: the Logan Mountain Lake. The Logan Mountain Lake sat just on the other side of a small hill near a town called 'Fishtrap.' Henry'd heard about this lake and knew that if they followed the shoreline north they'd eventually find themselves in Georgia and then Tennessee.

The further north they got, the better chance they'd find people who could help them escape.

They slept under leaves during the day and ate what they could find. Sometimes Henry would sneak onto plantation lands and steal vegetables that were growing in plantation gardens. Sometimes they didn't have much of anything to eat at all.

It had been days since they'd bathed so in the cloudy evening sky they stripped down to their skivvies and splashed at the shallow edge of the lake. The water felt wonderful. After they were both clean and refreshed, they waded out and sat on a grassy spot to dry off a bit before they redressed.

"Henry," Winnie said as she snuggled close to him. "Where's my Mama at? Where's Josiah?" She sounded so confused. Henry had already talked to her about all of this but when you're only seven years old things don't always make sense for any length of time.

"Winnie, don't ya worry none. Mama and Josiah's gonna be comin' behind us. We's gonna make sho' they's free too. They had to stay back a bit and take care o' some things, but don't ya worry yer pretty head none. They'll be along shortly, child."

Henry hated fibbing to her but he knew there wasn't another way. She was too young to know that she might not see her mother and brother again, and Henry couldn't guarantee anything at the moment. He wasn't even sure they'd make it to Ohio themselves.

"I jus' miss Mama so much, Henry," Winnie said softly and she leaned more deeply into his arm.

"I know ya does, Winnie. But I'm here for ya. I'll take care o' ya." Henry held the little girl close.

Chapter Fifteen

By the time the sun was beginning to rise over the water, Winnie and Henry had made it to a small inlet. There, Henry was able to catch a couple of catfish and cook them over a fire he'd made. It was the best catfish they'd ever eaten. Henry was glad they were traveling beside the lake because there were plenty of places to hide if it became necessary, and plenty of fish to eat.

They found a grouping of fallen trees a couple hundred yards away from the water and beneath a canopy of thick timber. Henry set down the blanket he'd brought for Winnie to lay upon and then made sure she was well hidden from anybody who might wander nearby. He waited for her to fall asleep and then tucked himself in and closed his eyes as well.

I found that I could talk to Henry easier when he was sleepin'. When his mind was off his worries and he could kinda stretch back and be his self. It was like I could see him standin' in front o' me and I'd reach over and pull him in close.

"Henry, I's so proud o' ya. I know'd ya didn't wanna leave Mama an' Josiah behind, but you's savin' Winnie from that monster and I's always gonna be grateful."

Henry looked at me and smiled. "I was gonna leave anyways, Delia – but ya know I'd do whatever I could to help yer family. They's jus' like my own." Henry took my hands. "I misses ya, Delia. I's so glad you comes to visit me like this though."

"Me too, Henry. I tol' ya we'd always be together, didn't I?" I pulled him to me and I hugged him.

Just then there was dogs barkin'. Henry and I parted and looked around. I couldn't remember ever hearin' dogs barkin' before and it felt kinda scary.

Henry heard the dogs too – off in the distance. His eyes shot open, and he realized they weren't in the magical place where he and Delia had been meeting. Those dogs were nearby and he had to get Winnie to a safe place.

"Winnie," Henry whispered as he gently shook the little girl. "Winnie, shhhhh." He put his finger in front of his lips. "You gots to be quiet. We cain't talk. Jus' git up and follow me."

She knew what was happening. Henry had talked to her about the things that could happen and what they needed to do.

The dogs were still pretty far off but getting a lot closer. Their barking felt like nails going into Henry's head and he was really frightened. Henry grabbed their meager belongings and took Winnie's hand. They ran as fast and as quietly as they could to the lake's edge. Moving into the water, Henry held the little girl at his waist and waded as deeply as he could into the warm tributary.

Moving along the edge of the lake he drudged as quickly as he could while staying mostly submerged in the slow-moving water. The sound of the dog's barking was now mixed with the sound of several men's muffled voices. These *had* to be bounty hunters looking for escaped slaves. Henry hoped they weren't looking for him but there was a good possibility of that, and he couldn't risk it.

Winnie hung onto their bag of belongings and onto Henry's neck. She was tense but knew not to say anything. He could only imagine how frightened she was but there wasn't much time to consider such things. Right now, he just had to get far enough up river that the dogs would not only lose their scent but they wouldn't be seen by the bounty hunters either.

Just then, he heard a sound coming from above them. "Pssst..." He looked up and saw a young white boy pointing to a group of rocks that were up ahead. He nodded.

Henry nodded a thank you to the child in return. He had no idea what was behind those rocks but he knew that the boy was helping them.

As he rounded the side of the biggest of the rocks he could see that there was a small area where he and Winnie could hide. It was almost like a cave but still in the water within the lake. There was no need to go ashore – no need to be concerned that anyone would pick up their scent. He hoped that from the shoreline the little cavern could not be seen. He reckoned, though, that with so many rocks sitting so close together, and with the space they were hiding in so small, it was likely that if they could stay quiet and still the danger would pass.

The dogs were getting louder. He heard one of the men yell, "I think he's picked up on a scent." Some of them were saying, "Over here..." and he could hear their feet running along the shore. Winnie held on even more tightly. At one point it sounded like they were right beside their hiding place. Henry closed his eyes really tight. He prayed silently, "Please keep us safe."

It seemed like forever but finally the men and the dogs faded away. As their voices and barking became less audible, Henry's muscles softened a bit. Winnie, who had been holding on tightly to Henry, pulled away a little and looked around.

Henry smiled at her. She smiled back. They waited a little while longer and then slowly waded out of the lake and onto the shore. Neither of them talked for a while. They were glad for the warm summertime sunshine because it would dry them quickly. Henry spread out their belongings on one of the rocks closer to the shoreline so they might dry as well.

Just then, they saw the little boy who had saved their lives. He was standing fifty feet away from them and peeking out from behind a big willow tree. He waved to them both with a smile on his face, and walked away.

Chapter Sixteen

Many days and nights followed their close call by the edge of the lake. They traveled at night when the North Star could guide them, and rested during the day when moving about was far more dangerous. They ate fish and wild berries and sometimes apples when Henry could find them. Mostly, they stayed by the river. Although the journey was a long one, it wasn't without its joy as well.

Henry had a lot of time to get to know Winnie. There was so much about her that reminded him of Delia. He found himself remembering games that they had played when they were young. In those moments he missed Delia; however it helped him find a way to play with Winnie to keep her spirits up. He was like a big brother to her, and for now, he was the only family she had. He didn't take that responsibility lightly.

It was about four days later that they neared the town of Stemley, Alabama. Stemley was also on the lake but was much larger than any of the towns they had passed by before. This made Henry a little nervous. He was also hopeful, however, that they might run into some people who'd be able to help them along their journey.

Stemley was due east of Birmingham – one of Alabama's largest cities, and there was much traffic going through Stemley and on to Atlanta, Georgia even further east.

As they began to pass farms and plantations Henry decided that they needed to be very careful. Strong, healthy slaves who were in their reproductive years and were able to work long hours were worth a lot of money. Even free slaves were often captured and sold for a good price in the south. The impending war didn't change most southerner's thoughts about the worth of having slave labor and good deals could be made for a young, sturdy man and a young black girl.

As Henry and Winnie traveled along the edge of the enormous lake, they came to a place where there wasn't any way of going forward without going through the town itself which was situated on the edge of the Logan Mountain Lake.

One morning, while Winnie slept in a safe place, Henry snuck to the edge of town, climbed a tree, and watched where most of the activity took place. He watched the people. He looked for other black folks who might be willing to help them. He looked for signs that the railroad was active in this place. It had been nearly a week since they left the plantation. Henry had no idea how long they'd need to travel or how far, but he knew they were only in the beginning leg of the journey. He was dedicated to making sure they arrived in Ohio safely but also knew he'd need help if the journey was going to be a successful one.

As Henry observed the layout of the town and the flow of traffic within, he noticed a house by the lake that had a small yard. There was clean laundry hanging on clothes lines in the yard and an older white woman moving slowly near a hen house.

It was while watching this kindly woman that Henry first noticed something very colorful hanging in the window of the house. At first he thought it was a curtain. Squinting his eyes to see more clearly, he realized that it was a quilt.

The quilt's pattern was of a yellow sailboat with a red sail on blue water. The sky was dark with tiny white dots – a night sky. He'd heard about the signs of the Underground Railroad – songs, markings on trees, secret nods from passers by and he'd heard about the secret codes of quilts. There was no way of knowing if this quilt was a sign to fleeing slaves or just a window dressing, but the boat on water at night made him think that the old lady was telling him that there was a way to travel north by boat and that she knew where he could find it.

His heart beat quickly with hope and anticipation. He climbed down out of the tree and went back to check on Winnie. Once he saw the little girl was sleeping soundly, he went back down the shoreline just out of sight of the old woman who was still cleaning up the yard outside the henhouse.

He watched her for a few minutes. There didn't seem to be anyone else around and he had to consider that his presence might cause the old lady to scream for help. If that was so, Henry might be caught and Winnie would be lost in the woods and on her own.

The old woman moved toward the well and began pumping into a tin bucket. Henry slowly moved out from the tree line. His movements were selected cautiously. He wanted to move toward her quietly but without any kind of intimidation.

The morning sun was bright. The sound of the water near the shore was a soft, lumbering sigh to Henry's ears. Still, he was tense with fear and watchful of any other movement outside of the old woman who had just finished pumping.

He paused, wondering if he were making a mistake trying to speak with the old lady. Just then, however, she looked his way. His eyes got big and he was frozen in his tracks. In that moment he realized that he had found his way to good fortune or really bad luck.

The old lady simply nodded a couple of times, looked around and put down her bucket. She motioned for him to follow her around the back of the house. He did.

Behind the house was a garden of vegetables and summer flowers. The hedges along the rim of the gardens allowed for a good amount of privacy. As the old woman neared a shed in the back of the house, she stopped and turned toward Henry. In a hushed whisper she said to him, "Boy, if'n you's lookin' to go north, meet me here tonight when the moon is high in the sky. There'll be boat to take ya up river."

"Yes, Maam. I'll be here," Henry murmured back. "Thank ya, Maam." And then Henry remembered Winnie. "I has a small child with me too. Is that okay?"

"It sho' is, boy. You jus' be here." And the old woman turned and walked away.

Henry carefully ran back into the woods and finding Winnie sweetly sleeping, laid down beside her and said to Delia, "We's on our way now, Delia. We's on our way."

And he closed his eyes.

Chapter Seventeen

Henry was sleepin' so soundly he wasn't even dreamin' so it was hard for me to talk to him. But Winnie was a different story. I watched her pickin' daisy's in her dream. She was runnin' and playin' with Josiah and helpin' Mama pick tomatoes. I didn't disturb her dreams none because she was havin' so much fun. It was wonderful to see her laughin'. I was so happy that Henry'd found the old lady and the quilt in the window. I was glad he was smart enough to figure out what he should do.

As the sky got darker, Winnie started to stir. Before she could wake all the way, I leaned in to her and I tol' her how much I loved her. In a groggy state she smiled and I knew she'd heard me.

She sat up and looked around, listenin' to the tree frogs singin'. Henry was still sleepin' so Winnie got up and pulled down her britches behind a tree and relieved herself. As she was straighten' out her skirt she heard a noise near the water. It weren't no toad nor fish splashin' but a person. She was scared and ran back to where Henry was layin'.

I knew it was okay but I didn't know how to tell her, so I tried to talk to Henry before he woke up. *"Henry, there's a lady by the water. She's a slave too. She's also tryin' to git away."*

But Winnie woke him before he noticed my voice. "Henry," she whispered in a tense voice. She shook his shoulder. He woke up and lookin' at her face he knew something weren't right. He pulled her down so's she was layin' beside him. "Shhhhh," he said.

They both listened. Henry was holdin' Winnie close and I's glad to see him protectin' her – even though I knew they was okay.

Out of the shadows, Henry saw someone movin' around and I was hopin' he'd realize that the lady was jus' tryin' to git away like he was.

"It's okay, Henry." I said to him.

Finally, the woman came into view. She was about thirty years old and was dressed in slacks and a work shirt as if she was a man.

Henry sat up a little. "Stay here, Winnie," he said and getting up, walked toward the woman.

For a moment, she froze. But seein' it was a black man she calmed a bit. She was timid but I could tell she was strong. I think Henry sensed that too.

"What chu doin' out here all by yerself?" Henry asked her quietly.

"Same thing you is, I reckon'," she replied.

"Where'd ya come from? How long ya been travelin'?" he asked her.

"I been travelin' for near a month now. I comes from just south o' Mobile. I los' my son to some slave catchers a couple weeks back and I ain't turned around since. I jus' keep followin' this here lake." She had tears in her eyes but Henry knew she was a fighter.

"You's welcome to join us, if'n ya wants to," he offered.

"Us?" she asked.

"Oh, yeah." Henry turned toward Winnie and signaled she come over to him. She ran over with excitement.

"I'm sorry, miss," Henry said. "I don't know yer name. I'm Henry and this is Winnie."

"Pleased to meet ya, Maam," Winnie said. *I was so proud o' her usin' her best manners and all.*

"I'm Miriam," the lady said, puttin' her hand out to each of them.

"We's meetin' a boat in a bit that'll take us further north. If'n ya wants to come with us, I's sho' we kin find a place for ya on it," Henry offered.

"A boat! How'd ya manage that, Henry?" she seemed quite surprised and pleased too.

"The Lord's with me, I reckon'," he said.

So, Miriam decided to go with Henry and Winnie. I was real glad. Winnie'd have someone who could be a Mama to her and both o' 'em would have a man to take care o' 'em.

When I was a little girl, even when Master was real mean or the overseer was around, I still always felt safe if I had Mama's big arms to curl up in. Mama seemed to make everythin' better even when she was scared too. She'd sing songs with us or tell us stories. I remember always knowin' that no matter what'd happen Mama would protect us.

I was glad that Miriam was there for Winnie now. She'd be missin' Mama more an' more, and I didn't really think Mama or Josiah was ever gonna git away from Master.

When Henry, Winnie and Miriam started down the deer trail toward the tree line and the water's edge I felt real content.

Chapter Eighteen

It was late when they arrived at the little
house by the river. The old lady had told him
to arrive when the moon was high. Henry
looked up. The moon *could* be higher. He
wondered if the boat was there yet or if they
should wait. No one spoke a word. There were
a few people out and about but mostly the town
seemed to be going to sleep. Slowly the lights
in the windows were darkening.

They had eaten catfish and wild strawberries
before heading on their journey and Winnie
busied herself playing with a doll made of
sticks. They were comfortable.

Just then, Henry spotted the old woman
coming out of her back door. She held a
lantern with a very dim light. She must have
turned the wick down low so she didn't call
attention to herself. She walked down to the
shoreline. They could see the reflection of her
soft light in the water. It was too dark to see
her face.

After a few minutes she climbed the bank of
the lake again and walked toward the edge of
her yard just beside the fence. She seemed to
be turned toward them.

Henry waited. Was she trying to tell him
something? Was he supposed to go down and
speak with her? Miriam leaned toward him.
"What should we do?" she whispered.

Without taking his eyes off of the old lady's lantern he murmured, "Stay here."

Quietly, Henry stood up. The lantern didn't move. He began making his way out of the woods and onto the top of the grassy slope that made its way down to the old woman's yard. He moved slowly. The lantern still didn't move.

As he approached the old woman he saw that she had her finger to her lips. She motioned to him to come with her. He followed. She went back down to the bank of the lake and after looking around cautiously, she spoke, "The boat'l be here soon, boy. Where's the youngin' ya tol' me 'bout?"

Henry pointed to the timberline. "There's a woman now too," he whispered. "Does ya think they'll have room for her?"

"Sho' enough, boy; you go git 'em and bring 'em down here. Wait by the water. The boat'l be here soon."

The old lady turned to walk away. Henry stepped up to her and whispered, "Thank ya, Maam."

"Good luck to ya, boy," was all she said. Then she turned and went back into the house. Henry watched her. He felt so much gratitude he didn't know what to do. He had always wondered why white people seemed to be so mean to black folk. Now he realized that it was only ignorant white people that were cruel. There were a lot of white people out there who cared about black folks and wanted them to have real lives. It really humbled him.

He practically ran up the hill to the tree line. "We gots to go," he said in a quiet voice. "Winnie, do ya remember what I tol' ya? We's got to stay real, real quiet, okay?"

Winnie nodded yes.

Miriam took Winnie's hand and picked up her belongings. Henry slowly led them down to the river.

They hunched behind some tall reeds in the wet mud. They heard owls hooting and watched the night bats swooping over the water feasting on whatever insects were flying around. Fireflies speckled the water and nearby grasses with a golden glow. The song of crickets filled the air.

But the loudest sound was the beating of Henry's heart. He was frightened – afraid the boat wouldn't come; but even more than that – he was excited. He didn't know how far the boat was going to take them or what would happen after that, but one thing for sure – they were going north!

Chapter Nineteen

In 1850 Congress passed the Fugitive Slave Law. The law stated that in the future any federal marshal who did not arrest an alleged runaway slave could be fined $1,000 (which was a lot of money in 1850). People suspected of being a runaway slave could be arrested without warrant and turned over to a claimant on nothing more than his sworn testimony of ownership. A suspected black slave could not ask for a jury trial nor testify on his or her behalf.

Any person aiding a runaway slave by providing shelter, food or any other form of assistance was liable to six months' imprisonment and a $1,000 fine. Those officers capturing a fugitive slave were entitled to a fee and this encouraged some officers to kidnap free Negroes and sell them to slave-owners.

Because of this act, blacks – both free and runaway – had prices on their heads. It didn't take long for bounty hunters and slave runners to try to cash in on any Negro they could capture. Many freed blacks ended up sold to southerners and many others were killed trying to get away.

These were dangerous times. The fight to get to the north was barred by many dangers but bounty hunters were the worst. For this reason, when a small row boat drifted into sight that warm spring evening, there were no words spoken between the owner of the boat and the three young blacks who boarded it.

The sky was overcast and as they began their journey there was a sense of dread mixed with a sigh of relief. The rower stayed close to the shore line – never moving into deeper waters that would have been easier to steer in. He had handed Henry an oar and between the two of them they rowed for hours past what was mostly wooded areas with distant fields and a few houses. They passed a group of islands called the Capri Islands and bearing to the left headed toward a town called Dunrowin.

By the time they passed Dunrowin on the left the sun was beginning to come up and they needed to find a place to stop. Just across the river there was an inlet with several small islands that George (the white man who owned the rowboat) told Henry to steer toward.

As they hit the shoreline of the smallest island, Henry jumped out and pulled the tiny boat onto the mud. Both he and George helped Miriam and Winnie to shore and then they hid the boat under branches of trees.

Moving inland a little, the ladies went to take care of personal business while both men set up a temporary camp. There was obviously no one else on the island and though it was small, it was well situated with no property lines nearby with people who might notice a small campfire or hear their quiet whispering.

When Miriam and Winnie came back George pulled out a sack that had bread, butter, jam and some dried meat in it. Winnie's eyes got really big when she saw the jam.

George whispered, "Tomorra we's gonna row up to a town called Riverside. When we gits there, I'll tell ya what to do next. For now, let's have some dinner and git some shut eye. We'll leave again jus' after dark."

They ate the meat and bread hungrily and then spread a piece of bread with butter and jam. Sharing it, they sat back, and for one of the first times since leaving the plantation they were able to really relax.

Winnie cuddled up next to Henry and fell into a deep sleep. Henry wasn't far behind her.

By the time twilight came everyone was up and about – taking their turns cleaning themselves and packing what little they had. George told them that the trip to Riverside would take most of the night but that they were meeting a man there who would help them get further north.

Again, Henry was struck by the kindness and compassion of these white folks who were so willing to help them. Helping black folks was something one could get arrested for and yet so many of them didn't seem to care. They just helped anyway. The further into the journey Henry got, the more he realized how many hundreds of folks were willing to put their neck on the line in the name of equality and freedom.

When the moon was beginning to climb into the sky, George said that it was time to shove off. They quickly uncovered the rowboat, pushed it into the shallow water, boarded and set out.

Again, staying close to the shoreline both Henry and George rowed silently. There were fewer clouds this evening but, once again, most of the areas they were passing were relatively uninhabited.

The lake had turned into the Coosa River and the tributary wound like a snake back and forth. It would have been beautiful country by day. By night, it was utterly peaceful. With the moonlight echoing on the deep blue water Henry felt like he was in a dream rather than a life-threatening adventure. He let his mind wander to Delia and their many, many days near the water after Sunday school. It was like he could hear her laughing and, for a moment, found himself sitting there with a smile on his face.

God, it felt good to smile when he thought of Delia. It had been nearly four months since her passing and he still missed her like it was yesterday. Still, he was doing what she wanted – and what he believed in – by going north and taking Winnie with him. In that moment he was truly happy.

After many hours on the water they finally neared Riverside. Riverside was a small town – much like Fishtrap had been, but just a bit larger. As they pulled up to the shoreline, George told Henry and the girls to hide the boat and themselves until he returned.

"I wonder what's gonna happen next?" Miriam whispered to Henry.

"I guess we'll have to wait and see," he quietly replied. And then he asked, "Miriam, kin I asks ya a question?"

"Sho'."

"Why you wearin' men's clothes? I ain't never seen so lady in men's britches before." He was smiling at her.

She returned his smile. "Well, Henry, after my son, Aaron, was captured and I had to run so fast to git away myself, I decided I could run faster and hide better without a skirt. So I waited 'til I could and stole some clothes off a line in Prattville and tossed my own clothes. I kin dress pretty when I gits to Canada. For now, I gots to be comfortable and travel easy."

"Is we goin' to Canada too, Henry?" Winnie asked.

"I don't know, Winnie. I didn't think none past Ohio. Preacher man tol' me that I needed to git to Ripley, Ohio. So that's where I'm a goin'. After that, I don't even know."

They sat quietly for a while. The water lapped upon the shore as the night sky began to give way to an early morning hue on the horizon.

Just then George and another man appeared out of the woods. "Git yer stuff and git goin' with this man. His name's James and he's gonna git ya to the next stop," George said.

Henry put out his hand. "Thank ya so much, George. God bless ya."

"You too," George said as he shook Henry's hand. "God bless all o' ya." Then George pulled his rowboat out of the brush and pushed it back into the water.

"Okay," James said. "We gots to git goin' before the sun is up. Follow me."

Henry took Winnie's hand, and they all followed James through the woods.

Chapter Twenty

The trail they took was narrow and the covering of trees overhead was quite heavy. James didn't have a lantern so Henry, Miriam and Winnie had to stay very close to one another so they didn't get lost. They walked very quickly through the brush. After about twenty minutes James slowed down a bit.

He seemed to be listening for something. "Hush," he murmured.

They all stopped. They waited. In a few minutes, James told them quietly to move slowly and keep their wits about them. He led them out of the woods. In front of them stood a large meadow and as the sun was beginning to rise high in the sky they moved through the tall grasses and butterfly weed that filled the meadow with life. They heard the sound of a rooster singing his morning song and wind chimes somewhere up ahead.

Finally a farmhouse, barn and large shed came into view. The house had a single lantern in the window and even though the sun was rising higher in the sky the whole time, the light in the pane was very welcoming.

James ushered the whole lot of them into a back door.

The kitchen inside the house wasn't large but held a big stove, wooden table that sat six people, and a sink with an inside pump for water. There were cupboards filled with plates and a large pile of wood in the corner. Upon one wall there was a wooden plaque with a carved picture of an angel on it and beneath it the words burned into the wood, "Swing Low, Sweet Chariot." Henry recognized this as a "code" song. They had been taught to sing this song in church services. The chariot referred to in "Swing Low Sweet Chariot" referred to the carriages and wagons used to transport fleeing slaves in the early 19th century. Henry knew right away that the next leg of their journey would be in a cart of some kind.

A kindly woman of about forty came into the kitchen. She kissed James on the cheek and turned toward Henry, Winnie and Miriam.

"Welcome to our home. I hope yer trip so far wasn't too unnerving. We're goin' to let ya rest up here a couple of days and then we'll be takin' ya further north in our buggy. We have to wait until Saturday so' it don't look odd – us leavin' an all." She looked at them with genuine caring in her eyes. "My name is Margaret. James is my husband. We have two boys, Garrett and Samuel. They are eight and eleven. You'll meet them in a bit."

Henry spoke up. "My name's Henry, Maam. This is Winnie," he said putting his hand on the little girl's head. "And this here's Miriam."

"How do ya do, Maam," Miriam said. "We cain't thank ya enough for all you're doin' for us."

"Well, you're very welcome." She smiled. "James'l show ya were you'll be sleepin' and I'm gonna cook ya up a nice breakfast. After that, if'n ya wants, you kin clean up and git some shut eye." Looking down at Winnie she said, "How's that sound?"

Winnie just smiled. She was shy – scared. Henry spoke for her. "That sounds wonderful, Maam. Thank you."

"Okay, folks, let's git ya a place to settle down," James said.

He led them down a long hallway. He moved a bookcase away from the wall, and there was an opening big enough for them all to squeeze through. In the small closet room there were a couple of mattresses and a small window that was shaded by a faded yellow curtain.

"It ain't much, but it's safe. The outhouse is in the back o' the house and we's got a bathin' tub in the room off the kitchen. If'n ya wants to scrub yer clothes we gots a few extra things ya kin change into so's you kin clean up real good."

After sleeping on the ground under leaves and fallen trees, this room was beautiful to them. There were clean sheets on the mattresses and Margaret had placed a few violets in a jar on the windowsill. They made the room smell fresh and clean.

"We has to keep the bookcase in front o' the entrance to the door at night or if'n we sees folks comin', o' course, but Henry, I think you're strong enough to move if'n the ladies need to use our facilities outside at nighttime. Is that okay?" James asked.

"Yes, sir," Henry replied.

"Okay then." Just then a young boy was standing beside James. "This is Garrett. Garrett, this is Henry, Miss Miriam and Miss Winnie. Will ya show them where the pump outside is so's they kin wash their hands before we sits down to eat breakfast?"

"Sho', Pa," Garrett said. He stood aside as the three runaway's came out of their sleeping room and then, waving over his shoulder, he said, "This way," and led them out back.

Winnie used the outhouse, and then Henry pumped the water while Winnie and Miriam both splashed water on their faces and washed their hands. After they were done, Henry cleaned up while Miriam pumped.

For the first time they were able to clearly see the surrounding area. The meadow was a beautiful expanse of land that led to the tree line from which they had emerged. There was a dirt road on the other side of the meadow that passed by the house, and it seemed to go on forever. There were no houses nearby and no sounds except the morning birds, clucking chickens and the occasional bleat of a goat.

Winnie's face suddenly lit up as she got her first whiff of bacon cooking. She looked up at Henry. "Bacon!" Her eyes were big with anticipation and Henry laughed out loud at the little girl's happiness.

Miriam said to Garrett, "Maybe I should help yer Ma in the kitchen," and she walked away eager to pay this family back somehow for their kindness.

Garrett asked Winnie if she'd like to play kickball until breakfast was ready. Winnie looked up at Henry. "O' course, child, you go ahead. We'll come and git ya when the cookin's done."

And they went off to play.

Henry stood in the sunshine, closed his eyes, and turning his face up to heaven said, "Delia, I think we's gonna make it."

Chapter Twenty-One

Riverside was surrounded by rolling hills and thick forests of trees. Although there were a few farms in the town and a small central area where people met for church, to go to the general store or to have a few drinks in the saloon, it was mostly a quiet community. They didn't even have their own sheriff's office. If there was trouble, they used the sheriff out of Pell City which was just west of Riverside.

The biggest problem Riverside had was that they were staunchly southern and hated abolitionists. Since this was true, James, Margaret and their sons were taking an extra big risk harboring three runaway Negros on their property.

There was a clear reason for this, however.

James had grown up on a plantation in Newnan, Georgia. His father had been a wealthy land owner and had grown acres upon acres of cotton.

The most economical way of running a plantation was to use slave labor. Negros were not considered human beings. They were property. They worked for little or no wage, lived in run-down shelters and could be threatened into doing whatever a Master wanted by intimidation. Slave women were raped, beaten and sometimes bore the children of their Master. This only populated the land owner's asset list more.

When James grew up he was a child of privilege. However, the privilege came with a price. Every day as he sat looking out his playroom window or kicking a ball all around in his yard, he witnessed horrendous treatment of other human beings.

This was difficult because James didn't see the slaves as property. He saw children whose hearts were broken when their parents were traded to other plantations, fathers who were flogged to the point of near death, women who were dragged away and came crawling back bloodied to work in the gardens, and ghastly fear that he couldn't stand.

He asked his father why he was so mean to the black people. His father told him that "Niggers don't mean nuthin'. They ain't nuthin'. They's filthy shit that's only worth somethin' if'n they's workin' in the fields. Niggers don't have no feelin's anyhow." He said it so directly – without any thought to these people's personal experiences - that James was chilled to the bone.

Eventually, James decided to marry and moved away to his wife's family's homestead in Riverside. There he joined the abolitionist's movement and raised his own children to abhor ignorance, self-righteousness and hatred.

Garrett and Samuel Haney were bright, loving boys who had a clear sense of right and wrong. They had grown up harboring fleeing blacks, and knew the routine well.

If someone was coming down the road, Samuel put a brick upright in the window outside the little room where the slaves slept. This was a sign to them that someone else was on the property and they should stay quiet and not come outside of the room. Garrett was in charge of making sure his father was aware of the situation.

Margaret always made sure to practice a run through with any of her house guests and with the boys so that everyone knew what they were to do and when. It was a carefully thought out plan that had saved many a runaway slave's life.

The second night while Henry, Miriam and Winnie were staying with the Haney's they heard the dogs barking outside. Immediately Henry, Miriam and Winnie went into their room behind the book case, and James pushed it back to cover the opening. Samuel placed the brick at the window. He wouldn't move it until the company had gone. Garrett helped mother put away any signs that there had been more than the four of them at supper time.

With only minutes to spare, the boys sat down and began pretending to be in the middle of a checkers game, Margaret picked up her stitching and James grabbed his gun and a polishing cloth. They could hear the sound of horses and men's voices.

"Okay, everyone – deep breath," Margaret said.

The knock on the door was loud and menacing. "Jus' a minute," Margaret called as she stood up.

Opening the door she saw three bearded men who had obviously been on the road a while. Their clothes were dusty and they smelled like they hadn't bathed in quite some time. Each of them held a shotgun and none of them looked very nice.

"Why, hello," she said. "How may I help you?"

"You cain't. Is yer husband home?" one of them said.

"O' course. Jus' a moment." Margaret turned toward the kitchen. "James, there's some gentlemen here to see ya," she called.

James walked into the sitting room, his rifle in hand, and over to the door.

"Kin I help you gentlemen?" he asked.

"Sorry to disturb yer evenin', Mister. We's lookin' for some runaway slaves. We picked up their trail sometime back but then lost it again. They's 'bout eight o' 'em, far as we kin tell. We think they's runnin' from somewhere near south Birmingham. You ain't seen 'em no where's have ya?"

"I sho' ain't," James replied. "We's been sittin' inside all night though." James stepped back a little to be sure the bounty hunters could see his sons playing checkers. He noticed that they looked around a bit more as well.

"Margaret," James said to his wife. "Has we got any coffee to offer these boys?" He turned toward the slave runners. "You boys want a cup o' coffee and some cake? My wife sho' makes a nice chocolate cake." James knew that if he invited the men in they wouldn't be so restless.

"No, thank ya," one man answered. "We don't want to lose time on those niggers. Much obliged, though." And they turned and walked off. They mounted their horses and rode down the road.

James closed the door. They waited a while and then Garrett went out to use the outhouse. His job was to spy the road to be sure no one was around.

He came back into the house and told everyone that things appeared to be clear. They waited another half hour before Samuel took the brick out of the window and James pushed the bookcase aside.

The curtains in the house stayed drawn all night and if anyone went out to the outhouse, they did so without a lantern. The night sky was cloudy which, in this case, was good. If those fellows were still hanging around watching the house, they weren't going to see anything that would set off an alarm.

When night came, Henry, Miriam and Winnie lay down on their mattresses, James closed the bookcase in front of the doorway and everyone in the house went to sleep.

Chapter Twenty-Two

It had been a wonderful two and half days with the Haney's. Miriam and Henry had done a lot of work around the house and the farm trying to repay the kindness of these humble people. Winnie had the chance to play with the other children and had enjoyed making cookies with Miss Margaret. Some part of them wished they could stay.

The call to freedom, however, was thunderous within their hearts. They knew that they weren't really free while they were sleeping in a darkened room behind a book case. Real freedom meant walking the streets without fear of beatings or prosecution. It meant working for their own money, and owning their own house. By the time Saturday morning rolled around, Henry and Miriam were especially ready to get on the move.

They were going to a town called, Ohatchee where they'd meet another man who would take them to Cross Plains, Alabama – just west of the Georgia border. They didn't know where they'd go after that but they trusted that the Lord would help them.

James and Margaret packed up the back of their carriage with crates of lettuce, peas and leeks and asked Henry, Miriam and Winnie to hide behind the piles of crates. They tied the crates in to look as if nothing or no one could be behind them, covered them over, and then set off on the road.

It was cramped and hot behind all the containers. The road was bumpy and sometimes they felt extremely uncomfortable. They wished they could move a little so they weren't constricted quite so much. At the same time, it felt safe tucked away behind the crates.

After a couple hours of travel they felt the carriage rolling to a halt. They weren't sure if they were at their destination or if something else was happening. They sat quietly - practically holding their breathes. Henry was very proud of Winnie – she hadn't complained, even once – and seemed to know instinctively that she needed to be still and silent.

They heard James talking with someone. The buggy started to move forward again but much more slowly and they felt it bear to the left. The road was much bumpier and after a few minutes, James stopped again. Henry could hear everyone getting out of the carriage. Before they knew it, the canvas covering that had been tossed over the crates was thrown aside and James was speaking to them. "Henry, we're gittin' these ties loose and then you three kin step out o' there safely. Jus' be a little patient, though; we tied these tight to keep y'all safe."

Winnie and Miriam smiled. Henry was glad he'd be able to stretch his legs soon. It took a few minutes, but finally James and a Native American gentleman were moving the crates aside. James hopped up into the cart and helped Miriam out. Henry assisted Winnie.

Their muscles were sore from lack of movement and they stretched while they breathed in the clean, forest air. Margaret offered them a drink of water from a canteen.

"Henry, Miriam, Winnie..." James started. "This here's Tooantuh. He's Cherokee. He's gonna git you folks up to Cross Plains."

Henry put his hand out, "My name's Henry. This here's Miriam and Winnie."

"I am happy to meet all of you," Tooantuh said as he shook Henry's hand. "Do you have all of yer possessions?"

"Yessir, this is all we got," Henry replied.

"Okay, then. You must say goodbye to the Haney's because we must now begin our journey."

Henry, Miriam and Winnie turned toward the loving family who had housed and fed them these past few days.

"I don't know how to thank you," Miriam started.

"Hush, child. You three's been a blessing to all o' us. We'll never forget ya," Margaret said with a tear in her eye. She leaned in and kissed Miriam on the cheek, bent down and hugged Winnie and then shook Henry's hand. "You take good care o' these two girls, Henry," she said.

"I will, Maam. Thank ya so much." Henry turned to James. "I wish there was a way o' payin' ya back," Henry said.

"Henry," James said. "You jus' help other folks like you when the time's right. That'll be thanks enough." James looked at all three of them. "Good luck to all o' you, and stay safe." He turned toward Tooantuh. "I'll see ya again soon, friend."

And with that, James, Margaret and their sons climbed back into their buggy and were gone.

The Indian turned toward Henry and said, "We will not be leaving until the sun sets behind the mountains but we must get you to a safe place to rest. There is a small settlement back in the woods near the river. We can make sure you have a meal and a place to lay your heads. When we leave tonight we'll be on foot so it could take a whole day of walking before we get to Cross Plains. It is only about thirty miles but we must travel over mountains and some rough land." He looked at Winnie. "You ready, princess?"

"Yes, Sir," she answered.

They all followed Tooantuh down a barely decipherable path. He seemed to know where he was going and they trusted him as much as they possibly could.

"Tooantuh, sir," Winnie said to him. "What does yer name mean?" Winnie was really beginning to show some spunk. Her shyness was being eaten away by her crucial newfound courage. Henry was very proud of her. He saw something of Delia in her in that moment.

"My name means 'Spring Frog' little one. I was born when the blossoms came back to the forest and the tiny tadpoles were just hatching in the water." He stopped and looked at her. Stooping down at her level he said with a smile on his face, "And what does your name mean?"

She smiled back at him. "My real name is Winifred. It means 'Blessed.' That's what Mama said. It means I'm a blessing."

"That you are, princess," Tooantuh told her.

Chapter Twenty-Three

Just after sunset, having had a short nap and having eaten a good meal, Henry, Miriam and Winnie set off on a trail with Tooantuh and another Indian named Amadahy (which means 'Forest Water').

Tooantuh was a tracker. Amadahy was a hunter. Between the two, they had assisted nearly one hundred runaway slaves to Piedmont by way of what would, many years later, be part of the Chief Ladiga Trail.

They would pass through two larger towns on their way to Cross Plains: Alexandria and Jacksonville. Tooantuh knew a family in Jacksonville who would help them hide if Miriam or Winnie were unable to make the trip in one day.

The trail from Ohatchee to Alexandria was through thick forests and along very uneven terrain. Some of the time one of the men carried Winnie but most of the time she walked all by herself. It was apparent from the beginning that these two Indians knew the landscape and had planned well for the trip.

As they neared Alexandria, Tooantuh told them that they would need to be careful. Although the town wasn't large, there was a good concentration of confederate supporters who were actively acting to put an end to the abolitionist's movement. It was dangerous territory.

The plan was to travel on the northern edge of the town, zigzagging through the more populated sections, finally making their way to Leydens Mill on the northeastern side of Alexandria.

As they approached the outskirts of town, Amadahy (who had been carrying Winnie at the time) put the child down and told them not to speak again until they were through Alexandria. Even though it was nighttime, this was an area where slave runners and bounty hunters often traveled. Amadahy explained that they couldn't be too careful.

They journeyed through tall grass meadows until they came to a dirt road that ran the length of a large plantation. Cotton fields filled the area on both sides of the road. The crescent moon spilled softly on their path and they walked single file as quickly as they could for the next twenty minutes.

Just as they were nearing a place where there might be better cover, both of their guides stopped cold. Quickly they motioned Henry, Miriam and Winnie into the cotton fields on the side of the road. They all lay down close to the earth and didn't move.

Just as they were able to still themselves, Henry heard hoof beats. It sounded like two horses. They were not traveling quickly. Actually, they sounded like they were traveling too slowly. Something about that frightened Henry quite a bit, and he turned to look at

Tooantuh. His signal told them to lie close to the ground. As the men passed by them only a few feet away it was evident that they were tracking something – or someone.

"You see, Daniel," one said as he pointed to the ground. "Someone's been walkin' along here and them footprints is fresh. They's here somewhere."

The one called Daniel said, "If'n they's niggers we're gonna make a pretty penny on them black heads o' theirs. They's gotta be at least four o' 'em."

Both men dismounted. They started to look right to where Henry and the others were hiding. No one moved. As they pushed through the edge of the cotton field, both Tooantuh and Amadahy jumped up at the same time with their hatchets and knives waving. Catching the slave runners off guard, they attacked before they could be assaulted themselves.

The Indians were swift in their act and in just moments the two bounty hunters lay dead on the side of the road, their throats slit. It was a gruesome sight.

Henry lifted his head to see what they were supposed to do. Tooantuh signaled that they should stay put. With Amadahy picking up the men by their legs and Tooantuh their arms, the Indians carried the slaughtered men into the cotton fields and made sure they were out of sight. They covered the blood stains with dirt and took any staples they thought could be carried from the saddle bags of each horse. They stripped the horses clean and hit them on their hindquarters causing the horses to run back down the road from where they had come. Hiding the saddles across the field, Tooantuh finally told Henry, Miriam and Winnie to step back onto the road.

Henry picked Winnie up and hugged her close. "Are ya okay, Baby?" he asked.

Winnie only nodded and held him close. Miriam stroked the little girl's back.

"How 'bout you?" he asked Miriam.

"I'll be fine, Henry." She looked at Tooantuh. "Let's git going," she said to him.

They continued to walk down the dirt road until they came to Edward's Lake, which was just northeast of Alexandria and west of Leydens Mill. Here, they were able to sit, rest, eat and fill up their canteens. It had been over four hours since they had left Ohatchee and they were all tired.

After about thirty minutes, Tooantuh told them that they needed to get back on the trail. He was aware that Jacksonville was at least another couple of hours walk and they needed to arrive before sunrise if they were going to be able to stay with friends of the abolition.

This leg of the journey was through woodlands and the little group of travelers was able to talk more openly. This made the trip much more relaxed. Miriam told Winnie little stories that her mother had told to her when she was a young girl and holding her hand, Miriam walked beside Winnie a lot of the time.

Henry walked behind them. Tooantuh was in the lead, and Amadahy picked up the rear. Everyone felt very safe in their hands.

After a couple of hours, Henry heard a few birds singing in the distance. These were morning birds. The sun hadn't begun to rise yet, but it was apparent that it would soon. Holding back a little, he walked beside Amadahy. "Does ya think we'll be gittin' there before sunrise?" he asked.

"We are almost there now," the Indian answered.

They were climbing a bit of a hill and just as they moved over the steepest part of it, they saw a small cabin in the woods. There was also a small barn and, once again, Henry noticed the lantern shining in the window. That lantern must certainly be a code he would try to remember as they went further north.

As they approached the house, a small side door on the barn opened and a young man stepped out of the building. He waved them on and Tooantuh led them inside.

Chapter Twenty-Four

Jacksonville, Alabama sits on the edge of the
Talladega National Forest. Nestled in the
foothills of northeast Alabama, Jacksonville is a
town steeped in history. The land that would
become Jacksonville was purchased in 1833
from the Creek Indian Chief Ladiga. Because
Ladiga was a signer of the Cusseta Treaty of
1832 under which terms the Creeks gave up
their remaining lands, he was allowed to select
land in the county and to have his title
validated.

The town was a Confederate town – vastly
opposed to the idea of freeing slaves and it
could be quite perilous to assist runaways. At
the same time, there were also plenty
supporters of the abolitionist's movement in
town and, because this was so, there were a lot
of hiding place as well. Tooantuh and
Amadahy knew most of them.

Edward Calhoun and his wife, Betsy, lived in
the small house in the woods where Henry,
Miriam and Winnie were now sleeping. They
had provided a couple of stalls with fresh hay
and a couple of blankets. The whole group was
tired to the bone and slept deeply under the
safety of the Calhoun's watchful eyes.

Tooantuh and Amadahy talked with Edward
for a while before also finding their rest. As the
day wore on, the Calhoun's went about their
daily routines and let the small tribe sleep.
Just before twilight they made sure that each of

them had a place to wash up, and a full belly of food to take them on their way. Amadahy had awoken in the late afternoon and had gone hunting. He had returned from the hunt with several rabbits and a couple of squirrels. This was his way of paying the Calhoun's for their kindness.

By sunset the five travelers were once again on their way down the other side of the mountain and off to Cross Plains. They stayed on the western edge of Jacksonville until they were able to follow a deer trail moving northeast on the western edge of the Appalachian Mountains. Amadahy had told them that the trip would be about five hours without stopping. The hike was tough and many times the rough topography slowed them down a bit.

Fortunately, however, they were traveling through forestland again and there wasn't much chance that they would run up against opponents of the abolitionist movement. This gave them plenty of time for small talk as they made their way over the foothills of the mountains. By the time they stopped for something to eat and to rest a bit, Henry and Winnie had learned a bit more about Miriam and she, about them.

Miriam, her husband, Ned, and her son, Aaron, had been purchased by a very nasty man in Louisiana who had sold them on the block to a man named, Albert Anderson. Master Anderson had no positive feelings about black folks at all and had had each of them flogged as soon as they arrived on his plantation. Her son, at the time, was only seven years old – the same age as Winnie – and he wasn't spared the beating at all. Their backs were covered with deep scars. Master Albertson had also had them branded the second day they were in Mobile. Their chests bore the permanent scars of the Albertson trademark.

Life on the Albertson plantation had been very hard. The slaves were given two meals a day, and mostly what they ate was left-over scraps from the Master's table. His wife was cruel and his children were taunting. They often threw stones at the slaves calling them names like "stupid black niggers." It was a horrendous life.

When her son, Aaron, was just thirteen years old Master Albertson sold Miriam's husband to a man from Jackson, Mississippi. There hadn't been time to say goodbye or make promises to one another – he was just dragged out of the shack they lived in one morning and she never saw him again. She'd heard the Master's children laughing about it so she learned through their mockery what the fate of her husband had been. Her heart was broken. Aaron was angry. And on that very day, the decision to go north had been made.

Their trip from Mobile had not been an easy one, and when they heard the bounty hunters and their dogs getting close by, Aaron had sacrificed himself, telling his mother to run as fast as she could – that he'd run one way and that she could run the other. "They cain't chase us both down if'n we's goin' in two different directions, Ma," he'd said. Miriam had run as fast as she could. She watched Aaron run off in the other direction. She'd heard the men and dogs chasing him down instead of her, and she'd heard a gunshot.

She didn't know what happened but she knew she couldn't go back to see. There was a good chance they had only meant to scare Aaron with the shot. They wouldn't get any money for a dead Negro.

And so, Miriam had come the rest of the way on her own until she'd run into Henry and Winnie.

Chapter Twenty-Five

The area now known as Piedmont is a community that began in the early 1840's, located at the crossroads of two early post roads. Tradition has it that a hollow stump was used by the mailman to deposit and pick up the mail. This point received the official name of "Hollow Stump." Later a registered post office named "Griffen's Creek" was established by the Postmaster General. Major Jacob Forney Dailey of North Carolina came to Alabama in 1848 and bought land from the Prices family. History states the Prices were believed to be the first landowners here. Major Dailey named the area "Cross Plains".

When they were just outside of this beautiful, mountainous community several hours later, they came to a small lake called 'Lake Haven.' Lake Haven was just southwest of Cross Plains. Tooantuh explained that they would camp there for another day to rest. He told them that Cross Plains, like most other towns in Alabama was immeasurably against the abolitionists but there were plenty of supporters too. They had sent word ahead to a woman named Annabelle Lockert who would help them through Cross Plains and get them on the road to Georgia.

Amadahy went off to hunt as the rest of them set up a temporary camp and lean-to for sleeping. They'd been fortunate that the weather had cooperated thus far, but Tooantuh was sure it would rain this evening. Once a fire was started, Miriam took Winnie to the lake to wash up and change clothes.

"Tooantuh," Henry began. "I haven't had much time to tell ya how grateful I am. You an' Amadahy – I mean – I feels like you's savin' our lives." Henry suddenly felt very emotional.

"Henry, no man should own another man. If it weren't for their greed, all white men would know this is true," Tooantuh replied. "I am glad we can help."

Henry smiled at him.

After a short time, Amadahy came back to camp with a couple of rabbits and the small party of travelers ate until their bellies were full. Just as they were finishing the rain began to fall. At first it was light and rather refreshing as they sat under the lean-to, but a little while later the rains got much heavier and the wind began to blow. They covered themselves over as best they could but by mid-morning they were all soaked as if they had jumped in the lake.

The rains didn't end most of the day. They snuggled together to stay as warm as possible and Amadahy promised Winnie ginger root tea as soon as they could build a fire. In order to keep the little girl's spirits up, Miriam sang 'The Gospel Train's A Comin" and before long everyone was joining in quietly, "*Get on board little children, Get on board little children, Get*

on board little children. There's room for
many more."

When the rains finally died down just before sunset, everyone was wet and a little cold but warmed to the heart. Once again they built a fire – this one bigger than the last, and Amadahy went out into the woods to find some dinner.

There was a deep feeling of connection between these five people as they warmed themselves, dried their belongings and ate a good dinner of quail and fish. Amadahy made his ginger root tea, and they all felt satisfied as the brilliant colors of a beautiful Alabama sunset painted the clear, deep waters of Lake Haven.

Chapter Twenty-Six

I watched them all sleepin' soundly underneath that lean-to and I wished I could lay down with 'em. It would o' been so nice to hold Winnie in my arms and kiss her pretty little face. But instead, I jus' watched 'em.

"*Henry,*" I said, tryin' to get his attention while he slept. "*Henry, kin ya hears me?*"

Then he was standin' in front o' me again. He come again to meet with me, an' I was real happy to see him."

"Delia, girl I misses ya so much," he said.

"*I's always right here with ya, Henry. You knows that.*" I smiled at him. "*I's so glad ya has some people to go with ya. Miriam seems real nice and she's so good for Winnie.*" I smiled at him.

"You jealous, Delia? I ain't givin' my heart to no one else, ya know," Henry said real serious like.

"*No, Henry. I's not jealous. There ain't no jealousy in a lovin' heart. That's somethin' people figures out once they's away from the world. It's all 'bout lovin' – nuthin else.*"

Henry pulled me in close and held me. "I's so glad we kin visit, Delia. When you're here I knows it'll all be okay."

"Well, I's always here, Henry — so it'll always be okay."

Chapter Twenty-Seven

Annabelle Lockert was supposed to show up just before sundown the next day. Tooantuh and Amadahy helped Henry and Miriam pack their belongings. They gathered their own things and readied themselves for the trip back to Ohatchee.

By the time the sun was setting over the western edge of the lake everyone was getting a little nervous. Tooantuh knew that it was unlike Annabelle to be late. On the contrary, she was usually much earlier then expected. Although he didn't want to alarm Henry or the rest of the small group, he was very concerned.

Amadahy eventually went to the lake to catch a couple of fish in case they might need sustenance this evening. He had packed plenty of eatable plants for the group to take with them but since they were packed well, it made sense to eat the fresh catch instead.

As the stars got brighter in the sky it was obvious that Henry, Miriam and even Winnie were anxious.

"I do not know where Annabelle is," Tooantuh explained. "She must have had a delay of some kind. We will eat fish and wait." With that statement, he got up and began making a small fire. There was no room left for questions. Tooantuh didn't want any. He didn't have any sure answers.

Once the fish was cooked they ate in silence. It became very apparent by the time the moon was high in the sky that Annabelle was not coming tonight. Fortunately, it was a clear night. They laid their blankets on the ground, near the fire which Tooantuh had stoked, and slept for a while.

By the time the morning birds were singing Tooantuh had placed more wood on the fire and Amadahy had been hunting already. Two large rabbits were slowly cooking over the flames as Miriam took Winnie to the lake to clean up. Henry took advantage of their departure to ask Tooantuh what he thought had happened.

"I do not know," Tooantuh answered honestly. "I will leave today to go her house. Amadahy will stay here with you until my return."

"What if ya cain't find her?" Henry asked. "What we goin' ta do?"

"Don't worry for now, my friend. Let us see. Most important – do not let the women become frightened." As he finished, Miriam and Winnie were walking back up the path from the lake.

"I's goin' down to the water to wash up too, before we eats," Henry said to Miriam.

As he got closer to the water, and out of earshot, he looked up to the sky and whispered quietly, "Delia, you stays with us today..."

Chapter Twenty-Eight

Henry, Miriam and Winnie spent most of the day with Amadahy gathering a bit more food and repacking the things they had needed to use. The thought was that Tooantuh would be back soon with Annabelle and they'd be on their way.

As the day grew on, and the sun began to rest lower in the sky, even Amadahy seemed impatient.

"Henry, whys we stayin' here by this lake for so long?" Winnie asked. "I thought ya said we was goin' to Georgia."

"Oh, we's goin' to Georgia, Winnie. The kindly lady who's takin' us had somethin' she needed to tend to so we's jus' waitin' a bit, that's all," Henry explained. He hoped he was telling her the truth.

Miriam knew something was wrong. "Winnie, how 'bouts you and me go and pick some pretty flowers for Miss Annabelle sos when she comes we kin give 'em to her to thank her?"

Winnie smiled. "Okay!" Winnie took Miriam's hand and they walked along the trail picking flowers and talking. Henry was very glad for Miriam's presence. She had quite a calming effect on Winnie and was able to give the child the kind of maternal attention he'd probably never have been able to give.

As twilight settled in, Tooantuh came into view. He was on his own. Everyone stood up as he came near.

"Tla," Tooantuh said to Amadahy in the Cherokee language. "Yu-wi hi-la-hi, u-wa-sa." Roughly translated this meant, "*No. People go alone.*"

Amadahy looked at them. Tooantuh said, "Sit down."

"What's wrong?" Henry asked.

Tooantuh pointed to the logs that they had been resting upon. "You sit. I talk," he said.

Winnie sat on Henry's lap. He held the little girl close.

"I traveled to Cross Plains – to the house where Annabelle lives. Her husband told me that she rode off to meet us many days ago. He thought she would be back by now. He does not know what has happened to her."

Henry and Miriam looked at each other. "What do this mean, Tooantuh?" asked Henry.

"I have met with another man in town who can show you the way to the Georgia border but he is unable to go with you. You must go alone."

At first, both Henry and Miriam felt frightened. Then they both quickly remembered that they had traveled on their own for a good amount of time earlier, and had done just fine. Miriam, especially, recognized that as long as they knew the signs and the codes they could make it north eventually.

"You should leave as soon as possible," Tooantuh said.

"Yea, we's goin' ta leave soon as we gits our things together. Winnie, ya ready for an adventure?" Henry asked her smiling.

Winnie took Henry's hand. She put her other hand in Miriam's. "Wes goin' be jus' fine, Henry," she said.

Both Henry and Miriam smiled. "We sho is," Miriam said.

"We will take you further toward town and show you the road you must travel to meet Robert Madison. His house is a small white house with blue shutters. You will see a lantern in the window and a red hen house in the yard," Tooantuh told them.

Before long, the little party of travelers were on the move again. They traveled over rough terrain and through part of what would later be known as the Talladega National Forest area. The mountains were high and the trees were thick.

This part of the forest was close to a large logging area but, fortunately, traveling along the edge of the logging camps provided more cover than could usually be anticipated in a logging area because the woods were so dense. It took most of the night to reach a crossroad where the little group parted ways.

"Do-'da-ga-g'hv-i, (*Goodbye*)" the Indians told them as they waved farewell.

Henry, Miriam and Winnie watched them walk away. Without saying anything to one another, they turned and continued down the path. Just as morning approached they came across a small white house with blue shutters, a red hen house in the yard and a familiar, welcoming lantern burning in the window.

They all moved slowly through the yard trying not to alert the chickens of their presence. An old hound dog began howling as they got close and, for a moment, the small party froze in fear.

They saw a woman peek out of a window and then a very tall, thin man slowly stepped onto the wide porch and waved them inside scolding the dog to quiet down.

"Master Madison?" Henry asked.

"I ain't no master," Robert replied. "But I'm guessin' you's in the right place. You is the folks Tooantuh told me to expect?"

"Yes, sir – that's us," Henry replied.

"All right then." Turning toward the kitchen he called, "Helen, you gits these nice people somethin' ta eat." And turnin' back to the group he said, "You's hungry, ain't ya?"

"Yes, sir," Winnie said with a smile.

"I'll bet you is," Robert replied. Pointing to a corner of the room he said, "You kin put yer things over there. Come on into the kitchen and set down a bit." And he led them into a charming, bright kitchen with a beautiful quilt hanging on the far wall.

The quilt was mostly blue and yellow. It had small triangles pointing in all directions on it but one of the rows was brighter than the rest. Miriam looked at it, knowing it must be a code quilt that Mr. & Mrs. Madison hung outside to signal runaway slaves.

Mrs. Madison followed Miriam's eyes to the throw. "That there's called 'The Flying Geese,'" Helen Madison said. "We uses it like a compass to point north," and she winked at Miriam as she poured them a hot cup of fresh-perked coffee.

Chapter Twenty-Nine

After eating a breakfast of biscuits, sausage gravy and grits, Helen showed the exhausted party to a small space in the basement where she had laid down hand made mattresses of hay covered with thick blankets. It was dark but quiet and they fell asleep almost as quickly as they lay down. It had been a very long and grueling day.

In late afternoon Henry heard sounds coming from upstairs. His first instinct was to awaken Miriam and Winnie. He was frightened that it was slave catchers and the Madison's hadn't told them where to hide if someone should come looking for them.

But the voices didn't sound angry or questioning, really, so Henry tiptoed over to the doorway to listen a bit better.

He heard Miss Helen asking the visitors if they wanted some dinner (which was what they called the afternoon meal in those days) and how far they had come. It sounded very much like the conversation Henry had had with her and Mr. Madison only hours before.

He was cautious. Peeking up the stairs in hopes of seeing who Miss Helen was speaking with, he was surprised to see an old black man sitting at the table.

"We see'd yer quilt and we know'd we was in a good place," the old man said. His voice was scratchy and sounded very tired.

"Oh, you's in the right place, all right," Mrs. Madison was saying. "There's some others sleepin' downstairs. When they wakes up, we'll git ya some clean beddin' and y'all kin git some rest too."

They were runaways too! Henry was rather energized by seeing other slaves here at the Madison's house. He wondered how many there were.

Knowing he was safe, he walked up the basement steps.

"Oh, here's Henry now!" Mrs. Madison exclaimed. "Zeek," she said looking at the old man. "This here's Henry." Zeek put out his hand.

Henry smiled. "I's glad to meet ya, Sir," he said.

Looking around the room, Henry saw that there were four other runaways with Zeek. The old man started to stand up, but a younger woman put her hand on his shoulder. "You sit, Gramps," she said. "Pleased ta meet ya, Henry. I's Iris. This here's my brother, Matthew and his wife, Gert. And this here's they're youngin' Harriet," she said pointing to a toddler of about two years old.

Henry nodded to them all.

Mrs. Madison said, "Are the others awake yet, Henry?"

"No, Maam, not yet. I recon' they'll be wakin' up soon, though," Henry answered.

"Well, ya hungry, son? We got some dinner here and plenty o' it," Miss Helen offered.

"I sho' is, Miss Helen," Henry said. "Much obliged." And he sat down with the people who would soon become like an extended family to him.

Chapter Thirty

Because Zeek and his family had arrived at the Madison homestead later in the day, Mr. Madison had suggested that rather than moving on toward Georgia that evening they should wait until the next night when everyone felt well rested.

So at twilight the following evening, Robert Madison and the eight fugitives left Miss Helen and their lovely little house to begin a journey through northern Alabama to Georgia, Tennessee and Kentucky.

The trip took them through a small town called 'Old Coloma' and then into rock-strewn mountains to the outskirts of a town called 'Centre.' They were traveling through Cherokee country and Mr. Madison explained that once he left them there were plenty of signs that would lead them to more help. As they neared a large lake at the northeastern side of Centre, Robert told them that he had taken them as far as he was able.

"You gots to git across the water. Once you's across'd it, ya git yerself to a town called Cedar Bluff. There's a road there'll take ya to Fullerton jus' outside the Georgia border. You jus' keep goin' north and you'll find yerselves in Ohio."

Henry and Matthew, being the youngest males in the group weren't sure how they were going to get across the water or find Cedar

Bluff but they knew that the women-folk, children and Grandpa Zeek would be counting on their leadership and vigor.

As confidently as possible, Henry spoke up. "We sho' will, Mr. Robert," and he extended his hand to the man. "Thank ya." Matthew, following Henry's lead did the same thing.

"Okay, then. Good luck to ya folks. Stay low and look for them signs – they's all around ya," and Mr. Madison turned and walked away.

Being on their own again was a little frightening, but Henry was glad for the company they now had. More people meant more support. Of course, it also meant that it would be more difficult to hide. Grandpa Zeek couldn't move very quickly and although they could carry Harriet, Winnie was older and more difficult to carry for long periods of time. They had many more belongings as well.

"I thinks the first thing we oughts ta do is camp until tomorra night," Henry said to Matthew. "We kin git them settled for now and you and me could scout the area a bit lookin' fer signs. Grampa Zeek could probly build a fire if'n the lady folk and Winnie finds some wood."

"That sounds like a good plan, Henry," Matthew replied.

A little ways away from the shoreline there was a good size area where they could set up a small camp for the day. Tooantuh had given them an extra blanket and Amadahy had packed many edible plants to eat. Miriam knew there wasn't enough there to feed so many extra mouths for very long, but if they were careful and wise they might be able to find additional plants and, eventually, some food along the way.

While the others set up a place to sleep and made some food, Henry and Matthew wandered away from camp looking for a way across the water. Neither of them had much ability for tracking so they marked tree bark with mud to find their way back to camp.

Heading down toward the lake, Henry thought they'd soon see some kind of sign that would send them in the right direction for help. Mr. Robert had made it sound like it wouldn't be difficult to find help. Once they got to the water's edge, however, they realized that they hadn't seen any signs at all.

Tooantuh and Amadahy had told them plenty of things to look for. Henry remembered Tooantuh saying that in an unpopulated area it was more likely to see marks on trees – arrows or zigzagging lines to communicate which way to go.

"Maybe we missed somethin', Matthew," Henry said. "Maybe we oughts to go back the way we come and look on them trees again."

"Yeah, I reckon we should, Henry. But what if they ain't no signs in these woods?" Matthew asked.

Chapter Thirty-One

Back at the camp Zeek and Winnie cleaned out a good-sized area for a fire. Gert held Harriet on her hip as she gathered some wild berries that were growing close-by. Iris and Miriam gathered sticks and larger pieces of wood for a fire.

It wasn't time to eat and it wasn't cold enough to burn the wood for no reason, so when everything was set up, Miriam sat Winnie on her lap and Zeek led them all in a song: *"When the great big river meets the little river, follow the Drinking Gourd. For the old man is a-waiting for to carry to freedom if you follow the Drinking Gourd."*

"What's that song mean, Zeek? I hear'd it before but I ain't sho' what I's singin' 'bout," Miriam said.

"Well," Zeek started, "There's a story o' a one-legged sailor, known as Peg Leg Joe. He worked at lotsa jobs on plantations as he made his way 'round the South. At each job, he'd git real friendly with the slaves and teach them the words to this song.

"The "drinking gourd" is talkin' 'bout the Big Dipper, them bright stars up in the sky at night," he said as he pointed upward. "The old man" means Peg Leg Joe, and "the great big river" is the Ohio River.

"The second verse," Zeek continued, "tells slaves to look for dead trees that's marked with the pictures o' a left foot and a round spot. That'd be Peg Leg Joe. The third verse tells us to keep goin' north over the hills. From there, we's to travel along another river—the Tennessee.

"The Tennessee River joins another river in the song's last verse. Once we crosses that river, someone'll be meetin' us on the north bank and guide us on to freedom."

The tiny group sat quietly for a long time after Zeek told his story. Lost in their own thoughts they also lost track of time. Finally, Winnie turned to Miriam and said, "Where's Henry at, Miriam?"

"Oh," Miriam said looking up. "Well, I expect they'll be comin' back real soon, Baby Girl. How 'bout we git some things together for supper. You wanna hep?"

"Sho'," Winnie said feeling very grown up.

As Miriam, Iris and Winnie were going through the few food supplies they had and trying to figure out how to best ration them, they suddenly heard Harriet screaming as if she had been hurt.

Dropping what they were doing, they both ran to Gert's side. She was upset. Looking the child over, she was frantic to find out what had suddenly caused the child to scream out and to cry so incessantly.

"What happened?" Miriam asked Gert.

"I dunno. She jus' started whoopin' and hollerin'." Gert was beside herself. "I had jus' put her down for a minute to spread us out a blanket cause'n she was gittin' tired."

Zeek was standing beside Gert now. "Give me the child. Let me look," he said calmly but firmly. Trusting her Grandfather completely, Gert handed Harriet to him swiftly.

He held the screaming child close to himself. "Shhhhhh," he whispered in her ear. "Where ya hurtin' little one?" he asked her.

Her scream was piercing. Miriam, Iris, Gert and Winnie stood with their arms wrapped around one another – fear on their faces.

Zeek moved slowly and lovingly. Very gently he moved his fingertips over the child's body while holding her close. He hummed a lullaby as he leisurely examined her with his touch. When he reached her foot, she pulled back and shrieked even more loudly.

Realizing that Zeek had found the injury, Miriam reached for Harriet's leg to steady it while Gert inspected it. Sure enough, there was a welt of some kind. It looked like it could be a spider bite which made Gert very nervous.

131

"Do ya think it's okay, Gramps? Is she gonna be okay?"

"Iris, Gert, Miriam," Zeek spoke calmly, "Find me some lavender if'n ya kin. I'm not sure these woods has any but look. Also, bring me some warm water from the edge o' the lake – some the sun's been settin' on. I's also gonna need a couple o' sticks to splint Harriet's leg so's she don't move it too much."

He held Harriet close purposefully not touching her foot too much, but keeping it lower than her head in case whatever bit her was poisonous.

"Winnie, how's 'bout ya play pat-a-cake with Harriet. Kin ya do that for me child?"

"Yessir, I kin," Winnie replied with a smile. She played with Harriet, keeping her quietly busy until Gert, Iris and Miriam returned.

Miriam had gone down to the lake to collect warm water. On her way back, she passed a lot of old dead trees that had fallen with one of the last storms that must have passed by this part of the country. She knew she had to return to help Zeek with the baby, but she was curious to see if there had been any marks on the trees. Knowing Iris and Gert were collecting the lavender and getting a splint put together for Harriet's leg she looked carefully over the fallen logs.

After not seeing anything of a particular interest, she began walking back up the path that led back to camp. Then, suddenly, directly in front of her she saw an old tree with a circle painted on it and a foot clearly in the middle. It was Peg Leg Joe! A sign!

Miriam was so excited; she almost spilled the water trying to get back to camp.

Just as she returned, Matthew and Henry were beginning to make a small fire and finish carrying some larger logs for later on. They must have returned from the quest just after she left for hers.

"Miriam, good, you've got the water," Iris said taking the small pail from her hands.

"How's she doin'?" Miriam asked Gert.

"She's better. We found a little lavender and Gramps is grinding it up to put on her bite. We'll soak her foot first in the warm water."

"Well, that's good," Miriam said. She walked over to where Henry was working. "Henry, I seen a sign. I seen Peg Leg Joe's sign on a tree."

Henry looked up at her. "What do ya mean, Peg Leg Joe?" he asked.

"It's a song. You know the one. It's 'bout the drinkin' gourd. Zeek says it's a slave song that's filled up with signs. I seen one o' 'em," and pointing she said, "Jus' down over the hill to the water."

"Show me," Henry said. He turned to Matthew and said, "We'll be right back."

Down the path a short ways, Miriam stopped and looked around a bit. Once she got her bearings she walked a bit further, and sure enough, there on an old tree was a footprint with a circle around it. Henry reached out and touched it.

"But what do it mean, Miriam?" he asked.

"It means we's goin' the right way," she replied.

"But we already know'd that. Mr. Robert tol' us we was." Henry sounded a bit defeated. He hung his head for a minute. Then he looked out over the water. In the distance, on the land across the vast lake, he could see a light. It shone like a beacon.

The sun had come up only about an hour before but the sky was cloudy and the beacon of light was easily seen from this section of the woods.

"Do ya think that's a sign, Henry?" Miriam asked. She could see that he'd had a difficult evening.

"I don't know, Miriam," he answered. "Matthew and I looked all night and we didn't

see nuthin'. I's startin' to think we went the
wrong way."

Miriam put her hand on Henry's shoulder.
"There ain't no wrong way, Henry, long as we's
goin' north."

He looked at her. He nodded. And they
headed back to camp.

Chapter Thirty-Two

After having a good breakfast, they each laid down on their blankets for some rest under a hand-made canopy of tree limbs. Harriet's leg seemed to be feeling much better and Gert gently cuddled with her.

The men slept under a different lean-to than the women. Even though Matthew and Gert were husband and wife, it felt proper that with only two shelters made, they should sleep more discretely.

Henry had trouble falling asleep at first, but when he finally did he began to dream. His dreams took him back to the plantation – back to the river that he and Delia walked by after Sunday School. And then he was standing there with Delia.

"I's so proud o' ya, Henry. You's so brave and strong. And I's so glad you's takin' care o' Winnie so good."

Henry smiled. "I still misses ya, Delia. But I feels good 'bout what I's doin' too. Winnie's gonna be safe, I promise."

"I know she is," Delia told him. They walked along the river, holding hands. The water was real bright blue and the sky was so clear. It was mid-summer in his dream, and the fields were full of summer flowers – their scent was strong and inviting. Henry stooped down and

gathered a handful of bright-colored blossoms and gave them to Delia.

She smiled up at him. *"Why, Henry...isn't ya sweet?"* She smelled them. *"I loves them – jus' like I loves ya, Henry. I always will."* And just then, she threw the flowers into the river and watched them float downstream.

Henry was surprised. "Why'd ya throw 'em away, Delia? I wanted ya to have 'em when I couldn't be here with ya."

"You's always here with me, Henry. Jus' like I's always there with you," she said as she put her hand on his chest. *"But life goes on. And I ain't livin' no more, Henry."* She leaned on his chest, holding him close. *"But you is, Henry. You's livin'. And ya gotta live without me now."*

He held her even closer. "I ain't never livin' without ya, Delia. I loves ya more than anything in the whole world. I always will."

"I know ya does, Henry. But love don't go away if'n ya go on with yer life. It jus' goes with ya."

Henry felt Delia pull away a little. She looked up at him and her lips parted. He leaned his head down toward hers and kissed her lips.

And when he opened his eyes, she was gone.

Chapter Thirty-Three

It was late afternoon by the time everyone was moving around a bit more. The woods were quiet, except for the sound of bumble bees, birds and a few noisy squirrels. Henry and Matthew went down to the lake to try their hand at catching some fish. Zeek helped the ladies find some berries and dandelions. Iris gave Gert a short break and bathed Harriet, cleaning all the dust from the long walking they'd done out of her hair.

It wasn't long before Henry and Matthew returned to a good fire and a salad of dandelions and wild strawberries. The fish cooked quickly after Miriam and Gert boned them clean.

"While we was fishin'," Matthew began, "Henry and me talked about things, and we decided we's gonna make a raft outa fallen logs. We kin tie them together with the rope Tooantuh gave ya'll."

Miriam spoke up first. "I kin hep ya, Matthew, but ain't ya worried 'bout usin' that rope. What we gonna do if'n we needs it later?"

"Well, I expect we'll jus' have ta take the raft apart when we gits to the other side o' the lake," Matthew replied.

Everyone nodded. "That's good," Grampa Zeek said. "What kin I do ta hep ya?"

"Well, whiles me 'n Matthew gits the logs, you kin start to bind 'em together," Henry told him.

"I'll hep too," Miriam said.

"How long do ya think it's gonna take to make us a raft big enough that all eight o' us is gonna fit on it?" Gert asked.

"Not long," Henry replied. "But we won't leave 'til tomorra night. We'll need to rest before we set off again. We'll all start workin' now, and be back later for sleepin'. While we're at the lake, we'll catch us a couple more fish too."

So, the day went on as planned. Gert, Iris, Winnie and Harriet stayed back at the camp while the others went off to build a raft and catch some fish. They gathered more wood, found some wonderful blackberries and were fortunate enough to find some wild carrots. When Gert put Harriet down for a nap, Iris played with Winnie and then while the baby slept, all three of them sang songs and played guessing games. When it was time to light a fire, Iris let Winnie help lay the wood.

Just after the moon began to rise higher in the sky, they heard Henry, Matthew, Zeek and Miriam walking back toward camp.

Winnie jumped up and ran into Henry's arms. Henry held the little girl close. He'd been so busy lately he'd almost forgotten that

Winnie still needed his attention. With all the extra people around, she'd been kept busy and had been well cared for. Still, nothing was like "family," and that's what Henry was to her – family.

"How ya doin', Baby Girl?" Henry asked as he held her on his left hip. "You wanna piggy-back ride?"

"Yeah!" Winnie squealed with delight. Henry swung her up on his back and galloped like a horse over to the fire and then around it a couple of times neighing and snorting making the little girl giggle with delight. Everyone smiled and laughed right along with her.

Eventually Henry stabled the horse and everyone sat down to talk about the raft. Henry explained (with Winnie sitting on his lap) that the raft was just about finished and that they would be able to leave tomorrow evening after dusk. Everyone was feeling very upbeat and glad to be on their way. Now that they had seen Peg Leg Joe's sign on the tree, they knew they were traveling the correct route.

Before long, Grampa Zeek started telling stories about the old days when he lived in Florida before he was purchased by the Master he'd escaped from. He talked about his family and the church services they always went to. As he talked, everyone had memories and feelings that moved in and out of their hearts.

After a while it got quiet. Henry was staring into the bright orange embers when he heard Winnie weeping in his arms. "What's wrong, Winnie?"

"Henry, I misses Mama," she sobbed.

"I know ya does," Henry said to her. How could he help her to understand? He held her a little bit tighter, closed his eyes and silently asked Delia for help.

Then he got an idea. "Winnie," he started, "did ya know ya kin talk to Mama even though she's not here?"

Winnie wiped her eyes. She shook her head 'no.'

"Well, ya kin. I talks to Delia all the time, and she ain't here now, is she?"

Winnie sat up a bit. "How ya talkin' to Delia, Henry? Master killed Delia. 'Member, we buried her."

"Well, Delia told me – jus' today – that love don't go away, it goes with ya. I know that Delia is always here with ya." He put his hand over the little girl's heart. "When ya thinks 'bout her, she's right there, and she's lovin' ya the whole time." He smiled at Winnie. "That's true with Mama too – and Josiah," he added. "They's always with us 'cause we love 'em."

"But I cain't hear nobody talkin' to me, Henry. Does they talk to us too?"

"They sho' does. If'n ya listens, you'll hear 'em. You kin talk to 'em whenever ya wants." Henry looked up into the sky and pointed. "Ya see them stars, Winnie? Mama, Josiah and Delia all sees them same stars right now too. If'n ya talks to them when ya misses them, the talk'll bounce right off them stars and into their hearts."

"You said that jus' right, Henry," Zeek whispered.

Winnie stared up at the sky. Everyone did.

Chapter Thirty-Four

They all lay down to sleep in the early-morning hours before sunrise. They all slept soundly and by late morning began to rise and begin their last day in this part of Alabama. Miriam hoped they'd get to Georgia by the end of the day and as each one awoke on his or her own, the plan for the day was to prepare for the trip across the lake and then moving further north.

Henry and Matthew were making oars out of wide branches that had fallen from the trees. They wanted to be sure that they had at least four of them so that they'd move rather quickly across the water. Although they hadn't seen any people the whole time they were camped out, the fear of being caught was always in their minds.

Gert was feeding Harriet when she began to wonder when Gramps was going to awaken. "Iris, go check on Gramps for us, will ya?"

Iris walked over to the lean-to that the men had all been sleeping in and as soon as she tapped Zeek on the shoulder, she knew something was wrong. His arm felt as stiff as the wood Matthew was working on, and he didn't respond to her at all.

He was lying on his left side facing away from her. Holding her breath, she rolled him over. His body plopped over revealing a man who had passed on in his sleep. His eyes and mouth were half open, though his face looked peaceful.

The shock of seeing Gramps lying there like that made Iris jump back and scream. Everyone else dropped what they were doing and immediately rushed to her side.

For a few moments, after the stunned gasps, the only sound that could be heard was the breeze whispering through the canopy above them.

Henry picked Winnie up and held her. Gert and Iris leaned on one another crying softly. Matthew covered Zeek's body with a blanket and Miriam held Harriet close to her chest. The small group stood close to one another – each of them mourning the unexpected loss in their own personal way.

Finally, Iris knelt beside Zeek's lifeless body, took hold of his hand and whispered softly, "Love don't go away, it goes with ya."

Matthew decided to dig a grave for Zeek while Miriam and Henry continued work on the oars and the raft. Everyone agreed that they should still try to leave this evening – that Zeek would not have wanted them holding their plans off.

In the early evening, Henry and Miriam came back to camp and told everyone that the raft was ready. Each of them ate their supper quietly – remembering Zeek, and thinking about their upcoming travels.

After dinner they held a small funeral. Following a few words by Matthew and Gert, they all sang "Swing Low Sweet Chariot" and Henry began to throw dirt on top of Zeek's body. When it was covered over, everyone took stones and placed over top of the mound of dirt. Miriam placed a cross at the head of the grave that read, "Zeek - he died a free man." When Gert saw the words she fell into Matthew's arms weeping.

"It's okay, Gert. He's in a better place now," Matthew said to her.

"I knows he is, Matthew," Gert answered. "I's jus' so happy Gramps is free."

Iris held Harriet and looking down at the cross she felt a warmth radiate through her body. Free. Yes, he died a free man – not a slave. She smiled, and turning to Miriam she said, "Thank you."

Chapter Thirty-Five

There was an island in the middle of the lake. They were going to go around it. The directions Mr. Madison had given them pointed to a town called Cedar Bluff just on the opposite shore.

After breaking down the camp, the travelers made their way down to the edge of the lake. The two men helped the ladies and children onto the raft and then shoved off.

The water was still – almost glasslike. The sky was nearly clear, though there were a few small clouds drifting lazily through the moon-filled sky. Henry, Matthew, Iris and Miriam used the oars to slowly move the raft through the water. With four of them stroking – even though the lake was large – it was only about twenty-five minutes before they reached the other side landing on the edge of a large cemetery. They felt fortunate to have landed there – it was quiet and they were able to dismantle the raft without worry that someone might see them. They pushed each log out into the lake as each one became loose in hopes that the slow current would take them away. There was no need to leave any sign that someone had come across the lake on a raft.

Picking up their slight belongings, and with much of the evening still ahead of them, Henry led them up the hill toward the town. They remembered Mr. Madison telling them to stay on the eastern edge of Cedar Bluff so that when they went north to Fullerton they wouldn't need to cross the water again.

Very silently the group got closer to the edge of the village. It was eerily hushed and aside from barn owls and night hawks the only sound was that of their feet pressing against the earthen floor as they plodded forward.

"I think we should scout the area before we gos any further," Matthew whispered.

"That's a good idea," Henry agreed. "You ladies stay back. We'll be jus' a couple o' minutes."

The ladies, with Harriet in Gert's arms, and Winnie beside them, scrunched down behind some trees to wait for the men to return. Miriam looked around from her position on the ground for more of Peg Leg Joe's symbols but didn't see anything. They didn't speak to one another. They just waited.

In the meantime, Henry and Matthew snuck more closely into the village to see if there were any signs of help from the townspeople. Passing through Cedar Bluff, it was easy to see where the town's name came from. Cedar trees grew tall throughout the area and many were on the bluffs that looked over Weiss Lake. It was also clear to Henry and Matthew that this was a confederate town. There was a small building on the outside of the town that had a sign which read, "Nigger Jail." There were no windows in the building except for two slits near the roofline where air could come in. As they peeked around the corner of the building they saw a man sitting on a chair outside the only door to the jail with a rifle in his hands. Fortunately, he was asleep, but Henry and Matthew knew they had to get out of there quickly!

Quietly scurrying away from the building, Henry decided that they needed to get away from Cedar Bluff. He felt it inside. This was not a safe place.

Signaling to Matthew, they both went back down the path to the place where the women and children were waiting. When the women saw the two men returning, they stood up. Henry immediately put his finger to his lips in a "hush" position. Gathering their things, they swiftly moved back into the woods and continued their journey due east of Cedar Bluff. By morning they had found an area to camp. It was in a deeper part of the woods just outside yet another cemetery. As they settled in, Matthew's eye's grew bright with anticipation.

"Look!" he exclaimed as he pointed.

Everyone's eyes followed his finger. There, on a large cedar tree only a few feet away, was an arrow. It was light, as if the rains had washed a lot of the marking away, but it was still clearly visible.

"It's a sign," Gert said.

"Praise Jesus," Iris exclaimed.

"Well, I guess we knows which direction we'll be goin' tomorra," Henry said with a smile on his face.

Just then, Harriet started to cry. She was hungry and there wasn't much food for now. The adults knew they could handle it and Winnie had proven to be much braver than a little girl should have to be. But Harriet was still a toddler and there was no way of helping her to understand or to ask her to be patient.

Another fear, of course, was that someone would hear her crying. It was morning, and farmers would be up and about – milking their cows, feeding their livestock and tending to their farms. Although they were in the woods, they were very close to some farmhouses too.

Gert gave Harriet a few berries to temporarily quiet her but she knew it would only help for a short time.

"What we needs is bread," Miriam said.

"Okay, then," Henry replied. "What we's gonna have then, is some bread." Looking a Matthew he said, "You stay and take care o' everyone. I'll be back in a bit." And he walked off.

Chapter Thirty-Six

Moving along the inner edge of the tree line, Henry watched the shadows grow wider as the sun came up to the east. The day was cloudier than the night before had been. He was thankful because it might be cooler too.

Looking as far as he could, he tried to find a farmhouse that was close enough to get to in a short period of time. He was concerned about the children. They had a small amount of food but not enough to go another couple of days and the little ones needed to eat.

Seeing a silo just down the road he realized he was closer to a farm than he'd noticed at first glance. He'd need to investigate the area first, but hopefully, he'd find a way to get something to eat. He wasn't against stealing it. These days he was sure that God never meant for children to go hungry – just as he'd never meant for one man to own another.

He stayed hidden in the tree line as long as he could, and then he made a dash across the road and into a field of tobacco. He wished it had been corn or wheat – something taller to hide him better. Bending down, he moved as quickly as he could toward the barn. As he got closer he could hear people talking. Unable to hear what they were saying, he still knew that they were fairly close by. He ducked even deeper into the plants.

Then he heard a dog barking.

He closed his eyes and prayed, "Please don't let them see me." But the sound of the barking was coming closer. Now Henry could hear two men talking to one another excitedly as they ran after the dog.

Henry was trying to decide if he could outrun the animal when suddenly it was upon him. Barking fiercely, showing massive fangs, there was no way the two men were not going to find him.

The younger man got to Henry first. He stopped in his tracks. With a look of surprise on his face, he stood motionless with his mouth gaping open. He appeared to be about fifteen years old and had a pitchfork in his hand.

Then the older man got there. There was no doubt that he was the boy's father. Panting, he looked at Henry, and then looked around to see if anyone else was hiding as well. Looking toward the road, he said to his son, "Let's git this nigger to the barn," and he grabbed the boy's pitchfork and poked at Henry until he was forced to stand. "WALK!" the old man said.

Henry was frightened. He was also angry. More than anything, though, he was glad no one else had come with him – that he had left Matthew behind. They still had a chance to get to Ohio and they'd have a better chance with Matthew by their side.

"Run ahead, Peter, and open the side door," the old man said.

The boy did as he was told. The old man pushed Henry along with several jabs. Moving quickly, they got to the barn in less than a minute.

As Henry's eyes adjusted to the shadowy light that streamed into the barn, he saw three other young men inside cleaning out stalls. They looked at one another and the old man told one of them to get some water.

Henry couldn't imagine what the man was going to do. He'd been beat and tortured in many ways by Master MacDonald but he didn't know what this man could possibly do with water. He wondered if he were going to try to drown him. His heart was beating so quickly in his chest; he thought it might jump right out.

Pointing to a bench just outside one of the stalls, the old man said, "SIT!"

Henry sat.

The old man pulled the young boy named Peter aside, whispering something into his ear. Peter ran off out the front doors of the barn toward the house.

The other man returned with a bucket of water and gave it to the old man. Ladling out a large dipperful of water, the old man handed the ladle to Henry.

Henry didn't understand. He took the ladle. Did he mean to be giving him a drink? Slowly, Henry lifted the scoop to his mouth and sipped the cool water.

"Sorry for bein' so nasty out there, young man. You never know who's watchin'," the old man said. "How'd ya find us?"

Henry felt his heart skip a beat. Were these people abolitionists? Were they going to help him? "I was lookin' for bread," Henry replied. He handed the ladle back to the old man.

"How far did ya come?"

"I's from Kingston," Henry answered.

"Well now, that's quite a distance. You tryin' to git yerself north, I reckon." It was a statement more than a question. "Well, let's see what we kin do ta he'p ya. First things first, let's git ya some food."

The old man put his hand on Henry's back in an attempt to move him toward the house, but Henry paused.

"What's wrong, boy?" the old man questioned.

"Sir, I's real thankful an' all but I ain't alone. I's got a small group o' people hidin' in them woods down yonder, and two of 'em is children. I came lookin' for bread to feed 'em," Henry admitted.

"That so?" the old man said. "How many's out there?"

"They's three women, two little girls and another man."

Six more, eh? Well, now," the old man said. Looking at one of the men who had been cleaning the stalls he said, "Tell Mama to set seven more plates for breakfast, Ted." And he smiled at Henry. "Let's git those folks back here nice 'n safe like."

Chapter Thirty-Seven

Jed Carpenter and his family had joined the abolitionist movement after watching a young black woman beat to death for standing up to a white man who was trying to sell her children. It was a wake-up call that changed their lives.

Ever since then, about four years ago, they'd helped several runaways escape to the north. They had relatives who lived in Chattanooga, Tennessee so it was easy to travel between Gaylesville, Alabama, where they lived, and Tennessee as often as they wanted without anyone questioning their comings and goings. It only took about eight hours one way and if they left in the morning, they could be home by late that same evening.

Jed told Henry to climb into the back of the wagon and brought a couple of farm hands with him as well.

They went down the road until Henry told them to stop. While Henry went into the woods to get the rest of his 'family,' Jed and the two farmhands got off the wagon and began loading wood into the back. It was a good cover in case someone came along or was watching them. If a Confederate sympathizer saw Jed helping runaway slaves and he was turned in to the authorities, the punishment could be severe for him as well as his whole family. Death and enslavement was the price paid by many abolitionists as they sought to create a just society.

Henry moved through the forest quickly. When he saw Miriam and Winnie his heart leapt with joy. He picked up the little girl and swung her around and around laughing. Then he hugged Miriam.

"I found us help," he told them all.

And so, the small group of weary travelers followed Henry with their meager belongings until they neared the road where Jed was working.

After Mr. Carpenter gave Henry the 'go ahead,' he and Matthew helped the ladies and the children into the back of the wagon. The two farmhands continued to put wood into the back of the wagon for a short time more, and then Jed and his helpers climbed back onto the wagon and drove back to the farm and to the barn.

Once they parked outside the barn, the farmhands led the small group through the back door and into a large, clean kitchen. This is when they met Lenora Carpenter – one of the jolliest women they had ever known.

She welcomed them each with a big hug, kissing the little ones on their heads and telling them all to sit in the dining room because breakfast was just about ready. Jed, Peter and the three farmhands all joined them in a few minutes and together they said grace and then ate the largest breakfast ever!

"You folks looks tired," Mrs. Carpenter said. "Peter here is our youngest and the only one left at home. We has three other boys and two girls all married and four grandbabies too," she said proudly. "I'll jus' bet we kin find ya each a clean bed to sleep. How would ya like that?"

They all looked at one another. Beds? Real beds? "Why, thank ya, Maam," Henry said. "I don't know how ta thank ya."

"Oh, there's no need to thank us, boy. We's jus' happy ya happened along."

She took the group upstairs. There was a large bed for Gert and Matthew to share. Jed moved a crib from another room into their bedroom so Harriet could be close by. The room had warm green and beige tones with beautiful drapes and a large dressing table with a mirror.

Iris and Miriam shared the room next door. It was decorated in pink and white lace and had a window seat with a soft, satin cushion on it.

Winnie asked to sleep wherever Henry slept so Mrs. Carpenter gave them a room down the hall that had a big poster bed with a canopy.

They all felt like they had died and gone to heaven.

She showed them were the bathtub was and the outhouse. She promised them a good bath when they awoke but encouraged them to rest first. She told the group that if they wanted she could wash their clothes and hang them to dry while they were sleeping.

Breathlessly grateful, they each fell asleep in their skivvies and slept as deeply and peacefully as ever they had.

Chapter Thirty-Eight

The small group spent three full days with the Carpenters. Jed told them that he'd be driving up to Chattanooga on Friday morning and that until then they could help around the house if they wanted, but not to go outside except to use the outhouse. They had time to rest, time to repair the damages to their belongings and get to know one another even more.

They laughed around the fireplace in the evenings, and Lenora Carpenter led them in song by playing a wonderful square grand piano.

On Thursday evening, after Winnie had fallen asleep, Henry wandered downstairs. Everyone else had taken to their bedrooms to read, sew or sleep. His mind could not rest. He was excited to continue their journey in the morning, and grateful for their good luck in coming across the Carpenter family. When he walked into the foyer, he noticed Miriam sitting in the dark parlor looking out the window. She seemed deep in thought and he didn't want to disturb her.

She must have felt his presence, however, because she looked in his direction. When she saw him she smiled. In the moonlight Henry could see that she had been crying. Her cheeks were wet with slow-streaming tears.

"Are ya okay, Miriam?" Henry asked her.

Wiping her face, she sniffled a little and replied, "Yes, I's fine. I's jus' thinkin' 'bout my Aaron – wonderin' if'n he's okay. I misses him so much."

Henry crossed the room and squatted down in front of her.

"Seems to me that a brave and clever boy like Aaron's apt to be jus' fine – no matter what, Miriam."

She smiled.

"Thank ya, Henry," she said quietly. "Whatchu doin' still awake?"

He stood up and stretched. "I don't know. I jus' couldn't sleep. I guess I's excited 'bout headin' out tomorra."

"Me too," Miriam whispered. "I wonder what we's gonna do once we gits to Tennessee, though. I guess I worries too much. We's had a lot o' luck so far, ain't we?"

"The Lord's been kind to us, that's fer sho'," Henry murmured.

"I wish we could go outside and walk under the night sky," Miriam said. "We been walkin' under the stars for so long now, I kinda misses it, don't ya, Henry?"

He softly laughed. "Well, I'm not so sho' 'bout that, but I will say one thing - I misses smellin' the fresh air all around us, and the way the forest smells when the mornin' dew lays on the leaves."

"Mmmmm," Miriam replied.

A few quiet moments went by while they both looked out the window with their own thoughts. Then Miriam said, "Tell me 'bout Delia, Henry. Tell me what happened."

Henry's eyes momentarily went to the floor. When he spoke, his voice was soft and warm – it was as if the memory of Delia filled him with some afterglow that was very much alive within him. "Delia and I growed up together. We weren't on the same plantations but our Mama's knew each other and so we was good friends too. We played together. We laughed together. And on the day she died, jus' before her Master beat her to death - I asked her to marry me."

"Oh, Henry," Miriam said as she placed her hand on his arm. "I'm so sorry. I knew ya was close but I don't guess I reckoned that ya was gittin' hitched to her."

"We always thought we'd be together 'til we was old and grey. We thought we'd have children and grandbabies too. But we wasn't careful sometimes. We'd sneak out to see each other when we wasn't suppose to be doin' that." Henry paused for a minute. When he continued, his face expressed the pain of losing the love of his life, anger at the man who took

161

her life, and guilt that he couldn't have stopped it somehow.

"The day she died, we met out front – there was a section of the front yard that was thick with trees. We met there. That's when I asked her..." Tears filled his eyes.

"Henry, I's sorry I asked. This is too painful for ya. I didn't mean to make ya sad," Miriam said.

"No, it's okay, Miriam. I know we haven't known each other a long time but with all we's been through, it's good ya know," Henry said to her. "Besides," he said putting his hand on top of hers, "you've come to mean a lot to me too, Miriam. You've been like a Mama to Winnie, and anyways, I sho' does like ya a lot."

Now Miriam's eyes went to the floor. Even in the moonlight Henry thought he could see her blush a little.

She looked up at him. She smiled. "I likes ya a lot too, Henry."

Chapter Thirty-Nine

They awoke early Friday morning to a
powerful thunderstorm. Rain was pelting the
roof and ground with a force that only made
the small group of travelers even more grateful
that they had stumbled across this generous
family.

Lightning lit up the sky with a brilliance that
was blinding, and thunder rumbled through
the floorboards like a freight train. Without
argument everyone decided to wait the storm
out. They decided that it was probably fast-
moving – as were most summer thunderstorms
– and they'd be on the road before long
anyway.

Lenora had patched any worn or torn areas
on everyone's clothing and had replaced a
couple of things with clothes their children had
left behind. She had given Iris a new pair of
shoes, Gert a lovely bonnet and Miriam a
blouse made of pink cotton with eyelet trim on
the rounded collar. Each of the men had
received new socks. Henry had gotten a new
pair of pants and Matthew a sturdy pair of
work gloves. The children were also well
provided for. It had been like Christmas Eve
the night before and Henry was beginning to
think of this next step as a whole new year.

But first, the storm had to subside.

Mrs. Carpenter, as was typical behavior for
her – being so optimistic and jolly – decided

that sitting around the piano and singing was a better way to pass the time than being concerned about the delay. So after a few chorus' of 'Old Susannah' and 'The Gospel Train's a Comin'" the storm passed, the sun came out from behind the clouds, and Winnie was the first one to notice the rainbow that extended right down the road they were going to be traveling on.

"It's a good omen," Lenora said. "Now, let's git packed up."

It only took about twenty minutes to get everything (and everybody) into the horse-drawn wagon. Mr. & Mrs. Carpenter sat in the front. All the other sat in the back with the gear. It was a covered carriage and everyone was safe traveling under the concealment of the canvas that was enveloped around them. Peter Carpenter and most of the farmhands had stayed behind to tend to the farm and the animals but Marcus, a kindly man who was himself, a freed slave, rode along side the wagon in case there was need of an extra hand (or gun).

Mr. Carpenter had told Henry and the others that the trip would likely take about seven hours or more. They would travel to Fullerton, Alabama and then cross the border into Georgia. While driving through Georgia they would pass through mostly farm and forest land. There would be a small village or two along the way, but generally no issues that might concern them.

There *was* a small Army post just south of the Tennessee border but it was slight. The Carpenters had gone through that area many times before while on their way to Chattanooga without anyone giving them any more notice than a wave. They held no concerns about questions that might arise.

The biggest challenge might come from the town which sat directly on the border between Georgia and Tennessee – Lakeview. From that point until Chattanooga there were nothing but continual small towns with a few farms in between.

Since this was so, and they were still deep in Confederate country, a back up plan had been put into place. If anyone *did* notice the small band of fugitives in the back of the wagon, Mr. Carpenter would say that they were his property and that he was traveling north to visit family who would need help around the house after an illness had laid some of them up. Mr. Carpenter's family actually had a large farm on the northwestern edge of Chattanooga in an area referred to as Moccasin Bend. It was outside the Chattanooga city limits far enough that there was little chance they'd be caught in the tale. If they were, they'd brought Marcus along to help. Besides, Jed's Uncle and cousin were also abolitionists and were aware through coded wire of the small party's approach.

The air smelled fresh as they traveled along the dirt road that led through mostly wild lands. Open spaces to the west of their carriage offered a view of slightly rolling hills and plenty of meadows and farms along the way. To the east of their wagon small mountains rose up that were covered with thick canopies of leaves which blew gently in the clean, summer breeze.

As they reached the town of Lakeview, Jed reminded everyone to be quiet. If things went as planned no one would ever know that Mr. and Mrs. Carpenter were carrying such precious cargo. Luckily both children were asleep as they passed down the main streets of the town and crossed over into East Ridge, Tennessee.

This was a bustling township where everyone seemed to have somewhere to go and something to do. It was fortunate that this was so because no one even noticed the Carpenter's as they passed through town and on into Chattanooga. None of the small group of runaways had ever seen a city as big as Chattanooga. They peeked through the canvas of their wagon and were amazed at the beautiful, tall buildings and wonderful scents of the shops they passed. There were also large, stately homes with gardens of flowering trees and roses everywhere.

With the completion of the railroad in 1850 a growth spurt increased Chattanooga's population by 60% - up to about 2,000 people. It was surrounded by rugged mountains on three sides; the city lay at the end of the Tennessee River Valley. It was an incredible view and they all sat in awe of the magnitude of the city.

On the northwestern side of Chattanooga they crossed over a wide river and then turned westward onto Moccasin Bend and the property of Master Harrison Carpenter and his lovely wife Helen.

Their home was a large, two-story, white-washed brick home with a shingle covering. There was a large grey stone chimney that rose all the way up the outside of the house and ascended high above the light green colored roof. The windows were long – floor to ceiling style with no shutters. There was a large open veranda that covered the whole face of the house and a covered balcony on the second floor that also wrapped itself across the front of the home and sat atop the veranda on the first level. Along the path which led to the enormous front door there were Azalea bushes, gladiolas and scadoxus. There were large weeping willow trees whose branches waved happily in the soft summer breeze.

As the small party arrived at the front of the house, Mrs. Carpenter turned around and said to them, "Okay, folks – we's here. Come on out and stretch yer legs."

Henry and the others slowly climbed out of the back of the wagon. The blue, late day sky welcomed them. A young black boy ran over to them from the barn. He smiled a wide, toothless smile. "Howdy," he said to them, as he took the reins and guided the wagon to the back of the house.

Helen Carpenter was standing on the portico. She was one of the largest women any of the group had ever seen. She wore a loud, purple gown that boasted a sheath of pale yellow lace. "Jed, Lenora – there ya are! Welcome!" She turned toward the doorway where a young black woman was standing. "Elsa, bring us lemonade, please. And ask Franklin to help Lucius with our guest's bags."

"Yes, Maam," the Elsa replied. She smiled at the Carpenters and the small band of runaways and then hurried off toward the kitchen.

By that time Henry, Miriam, Winnie and the others had all reached the porch. Helen Carpenter turned toward them. "Welcome, welcome – all o' ya. I'm so glad you were able to come!" She treated them as if they were guests in her home – which, of course, they were – but like regular people – not like blacks or slaves or runaways. "Oh, and a babe, too!" she gushed looking at Harriet. "Well, we're going to have so much fun, aren't we?" She asked them if it was satisfactory if they sat on the porch and sipped lemonade until supper was ready. No one really knew what to make of Helen Carpenter – she really seemed to want their opinion.

The group quietly nodded 'yes' and Lenora spoke up saying that everyone was just a little cramped and tired from hiding in the back of the wagon. Jed asked where his brother Harrison was after they'd all found a seat and Helen chatted with Jed a bit about some business ventures that her husband had gotten involved with. "But he'll be home shortly," she said.

Just about then, Elsa returned with some cold lemonade and a few small sweet biscuits. "Elsa, please join us. I think it's important that everyone gits to know one another." Elsa smiled, "Yes, Maam, Miss Helen." And she picked up a glass, poured herself some lemonade and sat down beside Winnie.

For about twenty minutes the group of travelers introduced themselves to their hosts, shared stories of their history and their adventures. Miss Helen was very funny but also very compassionate. Eventually the young boy who had met them when they first arrived and another young man who appeared to be around Henry's age joined them on the porch. They were both Elsa's brothers – Franklin and Lucius.

Lucius was seven years old and within minutes he and Winnie began playing tag together in the front yard. Everyone enjoyed the children's laughter and comraderey.

Franklin seemed to be very mature for his age. One got the feeling, when talking with him that he was that acting overseer on the plantation. When Master Harrison's horse came into view, Franklin immediately ran to meet him and take care of his saddlebags and the horse. He told Lucius to carry water from the well to water the horse, and expected Elsa to pour Master Harrison a cool glass of lemonade.

After warm greetings and introductions, an older black woman came to the door and announced that supper was served. They all meandered into the large dining room and Miss Helen asked them to please be seated. It was then that the small group of runaways saw the most shocking thing they'd ever seen.

The older black woman – her name, they would later found out, was Eunice, her two sons, Franklin and Lucius, her daughter, Elsa and her husband, John, all sat down with them at the table.

Joining hands, Master Harrison Carpenter began a prayer of thanks. In Henry's heart – in that very moment – he knew that everything they'd been through and everything that might still come about was worth it. This was what freedom was truly about. He bowed his head, closed his eyes, and gave thanks.

Chapter Forty

They stayed with the Carpenter family for a week. Henry, Matthew and Jed helped John around the farm as much as they could. With their assistance, Franklin was able to mend fences on the northern end of the property in one day.

Miriam, Iris, Gertrude and Lenora all helped Miss Carpenter and Eunice with household chores, mending, caring for the children, and tending the garden. They were very surprised to see Miss Helen working right alongside Eunice.

One evening, about four days after they had arrived at the home of Harrison and Helen Carpenter, the two brothers were sitting on the front porch discussing political policies and smoking cigars when Master Harrison turned to his brother and said to him, "Jed, they's a lot o' fightin' jus' east o' here. The war's on and it ain't safe for any o' y'all to stay much longer."

"I knows it," Jed replied. "We's plannin' on gittin' these folks on their way the day after tomorra."

Master Harrison, now speaking in a hush, said to Jed, "That Fugitive Slave Law's got me feelin' antsy 'bout sendin' John and Franklin ahead with the runaways that's stayin' here with us. It weren't so bad a few years ago, Jed, but now this family that's become jus' like our own kin in many ways could be threatened if'n the wrong person decides the whole group is runaways."

Jed didn't say anything for a few minutes. It was as if he was trying to absorb what his brother was really saying. It was obvious that Master Harrison was not only concerned for the family of blacks that lived on his property, but for his own family as well. Anyone who wanted to could lie and say that the runaways belonged to them. There was no way around the fact that if something like that happened, his blacks as well as the fugitives that his brother had brought to his Moccasin Bend farm would be punished or resold further south.

"Harrison," Jed started. "I knows you's scared for yer family – both o' 'em, and believe me, I knows how dangerous it kin be. I's a little worried every time I brings a black up here. Naturally, I respects yer decision not to put Franklin or John in harm's way. They's been with ya a long time."

"Thank ya, Jed," Harrison replied. He put a hand on his brother's shoulder. "We might not feel comfortable takin' 'em up north, but we kin tell 'em how to git there. We kin give 'em food and other essentials that'll help 'em."

Jed was slowly nodding his head but his eyes looked weary. His heart felt heavy. He had grown to care very much for the small group of escapee's in his care.

Both men were deep in thought and completely unaware that Miriam had been dusting a table close to an open window and had heard the whole conversation.

Her heart sank when she realized that they would be on their own once again. Not that they hadn't done everything well when they traveled alone but it was so much more frightening – they were so much more on edge.

She moved slowly to the kitchen. Deep in thought, she wasn't even aware that her eyes had filled with tears. She was frightened. She didn't know why, exactly, but it was as if some horrible danger loomed ahead. Perhaps it was the idea of fighting – guns, killing – or maybe she was just tired. It seemed like she'd been running forever. She thought of Aaron and wished he'd have gotten away too. She wondered where he was and if he was safe.

As she rounded the corner profoundly assessing the recent events of her life, she bumped right into Henry.

"Oh," he said, a bit startled. "I'm sorry, Miriam. I didn't hear ya comin' 'round the corner."

She didn't look up at him. "It's okay, Henry." She tried to move past him but he stopped her. Bending down a little he noticed a tear slipping down the side of her face. His hand reached to her arm. "Miriam, what's wrong?"

It didn't take anything more for Miriam to feel as if she was going to break. Henry could see that she was trying to stay in control but that something quite worrisome was bothering her.

"Let's go for a walk, Miriam." He put his hand around her shoulder. "Whatever it is, I'll help ya, okay?"

She didn't reply. She couldn't.

They went outside by way of the parlor door and neither of them said anything for a while. There were rose gardens in the back of the house and a couple of marble benches under flowering Rose of Sharon trees. The gardens were very private except for a couple of bluebirds who were splashing a nearby birdbath. Henry led Miriam over to one of the benches and encouraged her to sit. He sat next to her.

"What's wrong, Miriam?"

"Oh, Henry, I's probably jus' overreactin'. I's probably jus' tired." But tears were welling in her eyes, and Henry felt himself wanting to protect her.

He took her hands in his. "Jus' tells me."

She blinked a tear away. It spilled down her face slowly. "I heard Master Harrison and Jed talkin' on the veranda while I was dustin' a table near the window. I heard Master

Harrison say he weren't gonna take us north. He says we gotta go ourselves. He's worried 'bout the fightin' and the slave catchers. He don't want Franklin or John gittin' caught."

Henry looked at her. Still holding her hands, he looked away for a moment – taking time to wrap his mind around what she'd told him. He sighed deeply. Looking back into Miriam's eyes, he wiped the tears off of her cheeks. "Miriam," he said. "I ain't known ya long but I knows you to be a strong, able woman. We's been through enough that I also knows I likes that about ya." He placed his fingers under her chin, and turning her face up to look at his more directly he said, "We kin do this, Miriam. You and me. We kin do this."

Her eyes melted into his. His potency and belief in her strength made her feel much more capable – more powerful, and she found herself looking deeply into Henry's eyes and smiling.

Henry felt his heart warm in a way he hadn't felt for quite some time. He was drawn to Miriam. He pulled her to himself and wrapping his arms around her, held her close, stroking her head lovingly.

Miriam didn't think she could feel any safer than she did in that moment.

Chapter Forty-One

The evening before the small party was to leave Moccasin Bend, Master and Helen Carpenter had a wonderful southern barbeque. Their children and their grandchildren joined the celebration too. When the ribs had been eaten, and the pecan pies only a pleasant memory, Henry and Miriam decided to take a stroll in order to help digest their overly filled stomachs and to talk. It was a beautifully clear evening. Moccasin Bend was surrounded by a lovely river in the lower Tennessee Valley and it was on that warm summer evening, walking along the river's edge, that Henry realized that he was falling in love with Miriam.

As they walked, they talked about how kind all the Carpenter's had been, and how great it had also been to get to know John, Eunice and their children. Henry told Miriam that he had talked in length to Franklin that very morning about how wonderfully the Carpenter's treated them – allowing them sit down to dinner with them, inviting them to the barbeque, etc. It was then that Franklin had told Henry that he and his family were no longer slaves.

Henry had been surprised. He hadn't actually known any freed slaves.

Franklin had explained that two years beforehand, Mr. and Mrs. Harrison Carpenter had given all five of John's family their Freedom Papers. Freedom Papers emancipated slaves from their owners and gave them freedom to live and make decisions about their futures as they saw fit. These papers safeguarded blacks from out of state slave catchers. To protect blacks from having their papers stolen or destroyed, registries for these papers were established.

John, Eunice and their three children had chosen to stay on at Master Carpenter's farm and now received a decent pay for their hard work. They were considered by Mr. and Mrs. Carpenter to be like an extended family. The small house they lived in on the Carpenter plantation was part of their pay as well. They were given livestock and part of the garden for their own use. There had been no real reason for John and Eunice to leave and so, they had lived happily as a family of free blacks for just over two years now on the homestead their children were born to.

Miriam stood looking out over the slow moving water. She was quiet as Henry told her all of this. He could see that she was imagining how amazing it would be to truly be free. The full moon spilled over the water like a lantern in the night. It reflected on Miriam's soft features and Henry began to think how lovely she looked.

"Miriam, remember when we first met and we rode down a river jus' like this on a row boat with the nice white man named George?"

Miriam smiled. "I sho' do, Henry. That was the beginning o' a real adventure, wasn't it?"

Henry laughed a little. "It sho' was," he replied. "That moon hangin' in the sky sorta reminds me o' the lantern we seen when we was waitin' to go with George."

Miriam looked up at the moon. "Well, it sho' does, Henry. It's jus' 'bout as pretty too, ain't it?"

Henry took a step toward her. He put his hand in hers. She didn't act surprised or pull away. She closed her fingers inside his too. They stood quietly listening to the early evening songs of the wildlife that lived beside the river.

"Henry," Miriam finally began. "I been thinkin' a lot 'bout us needin' to go north on our own. I was real scared at first." She paused. "But then, I started to thinkin' 'bout it different like. Ya know, the things that happen t' us ain't as important as how we acts once they happens. We cain't control everything. We cain't even choose lots o' the things that makes us – us. But it seems to me that we always choose what we does with our situations. That might even be the greatest freedom we gots."

She looked up at Henry. She took his other hand in hers, and as they stood facing one another, holding one another's hands she said to him, "I wants to be free."

Henry looked into her eyes and felt the conviction in her heart. He felt himself melt into her. He bent down and gently pulling her in, kissed her softly.

And Miriam kissed him right back.

Chapter Forty-two

Early in the evening, the next day, with bright stars in the sky a nearly full moon to guide their way, the group prepared to get on their way.

John, Eunice and Franklin had packed essentials for the group. There were four satchels of dried meats, hard breads, tea, dried corn and apples. They had five canteens of water that Gert and Winnie would carry. Luscious and Elsa put in a couple of peppermint sticks. In addition Mr. & Mrs. Carpenter had made sure they had a good sharp knife, flint, a compass, a map of the area where they'd be traveling, and the name of a man who lived in Monticello, Kentucky who would be able to help them get to Ohio. Mr. Günter, who owned a bakery in Monticello, was an abolitionist, and a kindly man who was very involved in the Underground Railroad. The Carpenter's had often been able to deliver runaway slaves to his back door for further passage to Canada.

As the families said their good-byes, everyone felt afraid, happy and apprehensive. No one knew what the future would bring or whether this group of people would find their way to their destination. At one point Miss Helen offered to house them all until Freedom Papers could be drawn up. As tempting as that was, all of them knew that the threat was very real that they'd be caught, unable to prove their emancipation, and sold again down south.

They agreed that it would be easier to keep working north.

With tears in their eyes – Henry, Winnie, Miriam, Matthew, Gert, Harriet and Iris said one last farewell to the Carpenters, and began the long walk through the state of Tennessee.

They stayed to the east end of the river, moving around the town of Chattanooga. There was an island on the northern end of the city that allowed them to easily cross the river and move northward to Jamestown, Tennessee.

The area where they walked was mostly isolated. They traveled around the small towns of Redbank, Hixson, Soddy-Daisy and Bakewell. By the time they were just south of Graysville, Tennessee the group felt just about exhausted. They had been walking since late last evening and now the sun was just coming up behind a few bright Cumulus clouds. They drifted across the morning sky like ships on a vast open sea.

Henry and Matthew found a remote spot near a fresh water creek and the ladies set up a camp while Henry and Matthew collected firewood and caught some crawdads for dinner. Though they had plenty of dried meat, Miriam suggested that they save that food for times when they couldn't find any. Since they were so close to fresh water, there was sure to be plenty of food to catch. And she was right.

The crawdads were sweet and tender and everyone ate their fill. With a couple dried apples for dessert and some cool water to drink, everyone felt very good about their first day out.

Beneath the awning of leaves above them, they each laid down using their satchels as pillows and fell into a deep, exhausted sleep.

Henry awoke suddenly and looked around. He was alone. He wasn't sure where everyone else had gone, but even their bags appeared to have vanished. He couldn't imagine that they'd all left him behind, yet he couldn't explain their disappearance either.

He got up and began walking toward the creek. Perhaps they were down at the water with the kids. It wasn't far, and when he arrived at the water's edge there was no one to be found. In fact, he didn't notice any sound at all. Even the water in the creek didn't seem to be moving.

Just then, he felt someone behind him.

Turning quickly, he stood in front of Delia. He was surprised to see her. And happy.

"Delia! Oh, Lord it's so good to see ya! I thought I wouldn't see ya no more; it's been such a while now." He moved closer to her to hug her but she put up her hand telling him not to come closer.

"Henry, I gots to warn ya 'bout somethin'." She was very serious. *"You gots to stay away from Ripley, Ohio. You gots to cross the river at Aberdeen."*

Delia's voice wasn't as clear as it had been before. She wasn't as easy to see. In fact, she seemed to be fading and Henry didn't know why.

"What are ya sayin', Delia? I don't understand..." Henry said.

But all he heard was the faint whisper of the word, *"Aberdeen...."* as Delia faded from his view.

He looked around. Where had she gone? "Delia!" Henry shouted.

And in that moment, he awoke with everyone startled and looking at him. He immediately realized that he had been dreaming and had screamed out in his sleep. He shook his head trying to remember what she had said. It was something about Ohio – Ripley...something about Aberdeen.

He looked down at Winnie who had a confused look on her face.

"It's okay, Baby Girl. We's okay. I'll git ya t' Ohio." And looking over to Miriam he added, "And on to Canada too."

Chapter Forty-Three

That evening after they'd eaten dinner, the group of travelers gathered their belongings and began making their way through the farmlands outside of Graysville. About an hour into their travels, moving just east of Graysville, they saw a light in a farmhouse window. It was a lantern. Henry and Matthew told the women and children to stay hidden for a couple of minutes and went to investigate. If there were signs to follow, they didn't want to miss them.

Sure enough, there was a quilt hanging on the clothes line just outside of the window that held the lantern.

The quilt was yellow with a green zigzag pattern on it. Miss Lenora had told them about this type of quilt. If they were reading it right, it was referred to as "The Drunkard's Path." It stood as a warning signal to take a zigzag route to elude pursuing slave hunters and their hounds that are in the area. A slave spotted travelling south, for instance, would not be suspected of escaping.

"Whachu think we ought to do, Henry?" Matthew asked in a quiet hush.

"Well, I hates the idea o' goin' back and then forth but it's good we knows 'bout this. If'n we comes across folks we's worried 'bout, we kin always go south," he replied.

They went back to the women and children and told them what they saw and what the plan was. Before they continued to walk on, Miriam said, "I think we needs to consider somethin' else." Everyone looked at her with interest. "I's only sayin' this causin' I had to leave my son Aaron and keep comin' north on my own." No one said anything. "If'n the slave catchers come – especially if'n they comes with their dogs – we's gonna have to split up. That way, we's not all gonna git catched. Since we have youngin's, it makes sense we talks about this. If'n we's comin' into territory that's more dangerous, we cain't jus' hope we's all gonna make it, right?"

"Miriam is right," Gert said. Gert was usually pretty quiet but when it came to Harriet, she was more than willing to talk about what could be done to assure the safety of her child.

For the next twenty minutes they devised a plan of escape. If they ran into men with dogs it would be much more difficult to flee successfully. Without dogs they could run pretty fast if they dropped their belongings. The plan was for Henry to pick up Winnie and Matthew to pick up Harriet and run as quickly as they could away from the slave catchers. But if dogs were involved, they would split up into two groups: Henry, Miriam and Winnie – Matthew, Gert, Harriet and Iris and run two different directions. They would meet at the next town just north if they all made it.

With a plan in place, they began to move as quickly as they could through the dark countryside. It was mostly an unpopulated walk and by the time they arrived outside of Dayton, Tennessee a couple of hours later, they were ready for some water and a short rest.

It took much longer to travel with the little ones but they were so well behaved, the group considered themselves lucky. The path ahead seemed to be through thick forest and as Matthew looked at the map trying to figure out any easy way around Dayton, Miriam asked Henry to walk with her a bit.

After they were a short distance away from the group, Miriam said, "It's gonna be a couple o' hard days ahead, Henry. I knows we just left the Carpenter's house, but I's already so tired o' travelin'. Sometimes it just don't seem like we's ever gonna git north."

"I knows, Miriam. It feels like that for all o' us. But you'll see - real soon too. Master Carpenter says that soon as we git to Monticello, Kentucky, Mr. Günter's gonna be able to help us the rest o' the way." Henry put his hand on Miriam's shoulder. "If'n ya need someone to lean on, Miriam, I's always here for ya."

She smiled. "I know ya is, Henry. I's jus' gittin" frustrated. It's scarry knowin' that any minute some group o' men could come out o' the woods an' put guns to our heads."

"That ain't gonna happen, Miriam. It jus' ain't."

Miriam sighed deeply. She looked up at Henry and there was something about the conviction of his words that made her feel a little better.

"Okay, then," she said. "Let's see what Matthew's come up with."

They walked back to the temporary camp together.

"Hey, Henry," Matthew said as they arrived back. "I been lookin' this map over good and it looks like we's gonna have to head a bit northwest once we gits to a town called 'Spring City.' After that, we's gonna have to travel for a while without any signs on this here map o' a good water source 'til we gits to Jamestown." I'm thinkin' we ought to fill up our canteens in the pond back yonder. There was a spring goin' into it and the water ought to be pretty clear if'n we catches it goin' in."

"Sounds good, Matthew," Henry said. "We'll run back there, fill up the canteens and be back in jus' a few minutes."

Miriam, Iris and Gert spent time playing with the children while awaiting the men's return. Within twenty minutes they had come back with full canteens and the group got back on the trail.

Matthew was right. After passing to the west of Spring City they traveled northwest for quite some time through thick forests. They walked on deer paths that were difficult to see. Under the covering of trees overhead the stars and moon did not shine through and the sounds of the forest animals frightened Winnie. Moving was slow and by morning they had only gone about ten miles.

Finding a place to rest, as the sun's rays peeked through the leaves above them, the decision was made to travel earlier in the day and rest when the night sky was its darkest. They thought they'd make better time that way until they were beyond the forest. Besides that, the fear of slave catchers in the depths of these woods wasn't a priority either.

That day, however, they were glad for the thick canopy above them. A storm blew up that brought with it a lot of heavy rain, strong winds and some hail. They were able to find shelter beneath shrubs and although they didn't stay completely dry, they stayed safe from the hour-long downpour that had ensued.

Three days and nights later, the small group of dirty, tired and hungry travelers came out of the mountains and entered the outskirts of a small town called Crossville.

Crossville is situated atop the Cumberland Plateau amidst the headwaters of the Obed River, which slices a scenic gorge north of Crossville en route to its confluence with the

Emory River to the northeast. Several small lakes are located on the outskirts of Crossville, including Lake Tansi to the south, Lake Holiday to the west, and Byrd Lake to the east.

SO much water! And for some reason, none of these bodies of water were marked on the map that Master Carpenter had given them. They were grateful for the opportunity to wash themselves and their clothes but concerned that the map they owned wasn't going to be as accurate as they might need.

Iris spoke up while the men voiced their concerns. "The map may not be perfect, but it shows north and it shows the city's we's goin' to. We jus' has to keep our eyes open and our ears perked up high like a coyote. We'll be fine." She sounded so sure of herself that she convinced the whole group to calm down and enjoy the waters of Byrd Lake.

And they did.

After resting most of the day in the woods just near the shoreline of Byrd Lake, and eating a good dinner of fresh fish and dandelions, the group prepared to (once again) travel through the night.

Taking a more northern direction now, they traveled past the small town of Grimsley before the sun began to rise. They'd made good progress and Matthew (who had become their navigator) told them that they'd definitely make it to Jamestown by tomorrow.

Finding a large group of fallen trees, Matthew and Henry made a lean-to, just like the ones Tooantuh and Amadahy had shown Henry to build. It was large enough that they all fit well beneath it and when the sun rose over the eastern ridge they stayed shadowed in the shade of the temporary shelter and slept.

Chapter Forty-Four

In the late afternoon they awoke to the sound of Winnie crying. When Henry pulled her close to him he realized that she was hot with a fever.

"She's burnin' up!" he exclaimed.

Miriam immediately stripped her to her bloomers and with Iris' help poured a canteen of water over her to cool her down.

"Matthew," Iris called, "is there any more water 'round these parts that we kin git her to?"

Matthew pulled out the map, and examining it, shook his head no. "I cain't see nuthin'," he said.

"If'n we don't git this fever down we's gonna have a real problem," Iris said to Henry. She held the little girl close. "It's okay, sugar. We's jus' tryin' to make ya feel all better, okay?"

They spent the next couple of hours hoping that Winnie's fever would ease up. Gert pulled out a peppermint stick for her to suck on – just to make her feel a little better. She didn't seem to have any other symptoms but by early morning she was still very warm, and she was obviously not feeling well at all.

"I think we needs to go for help," Miriam said. "I's goin'."

"You ain't goin' no where, Miriam. I'll go," Henry told her.

But Winnie began to cry, "Please don't leave me, Henry..."

Miriam looked at him sternly. "I's goin'. There's a couple o' farms nearby. If'n I kin git help, I'll bring 'em back here."

"I'll go with ya," Matthew said. Henry nodded his head - thanking Matthew for not letting her go alone.

They left within minutes. Remembering that they had passed a farmhouse about an hour before stopping at dawn, they headed back the way they had come.

With the sun high in the sky it was much easier to traverse the dirt roads and pathways going back toward Byrd Lake. They didn't talk to one another. Both Matthew and Miriam were completely focused on finding help for Winnie.

After walking quickly for about forty-five minutes, they came across a farmhouse that they thought was the one they'd seen the night before. Crossing the fields as quickly as they could, they arrived near the barn in only a few more minutes.

As they got closer, however, they heard a man screaming. He sounded like he was in pain. Matthew told Miriam to duck down and he peeked slowly over the rows of corn that were just about as high as his chest.

"I cain't see nuthin'," Matthew said. "I'm gonna try to git closer. You stay here." He wasn't asking – he was quite firm about it, and Miriam just nodded.

Matthew crept very slowly through the corn rows trying to get close enough to see what was going on. It was then that he heard the crack of a whip. Again, a horrifying scream!

"You damned nigger," someone screamed. "You is dirt. You's jus' a maggot – a stupid, damned piece o' shit. Don't ya ever question what I says to ya again!" And again, he heard the whip, and then another blood-curdling scream.

Taking a slow deep breath, and moving slightly to the left, he peeked one more time over the corn. There, a young black man was tied to four long stakes in the ground. He was laying face-down on the dirt – both his hands and feet spread wide apart and tied tightly. He was naked and the man beating him was an older white man. The man's back was bleeding profusely and Matthew could tell he was close to losing consciousness. He had seen it too many times before.

Suddenly Matthew felt sick. Swallowing hard, he turned as quickly as he could and made his way back to Miriam.

As soon as she saw him she knew something was terribly wrong. "What?" she whispered.

He simply shook his head 'no' and guided her away from the farmhouse. When they were far enough away, and in the covering of a tree line, Matthew sat down against a tree and put his head in his hands.

Miriam didn't say anything for a few minutes. Matthew was sweating and when he seemed to be in some better control, she said, "Okay, let's go somewhere's else."

He nodded, got up, and they began walking further south. After another thirty minutes or so of traveling they came across a small building to the left side of the road. It had a sign beside it which read, "Church of the Harvest." They looked at one another. Once again, with no words they both began walking toward the small building. Surely a preacher would help them.

The Church of the Harvest had only a small congregation in 1861. The people in this area of the country were hungry to know more than traditional churches had to offer them. They were also burdened with a desire to make a difference in the world for the Kingdom of God. They took turns having Bible Studies, Worship Services, & Prayer Meetings in their homes for many years. After a few years more they had rented this small building to meet in.

As Miriam and Matthew stood at the doorway of the building that was being used for the meetings they felt hopeful, frightened and worried.

It was Miriam who finally knocked on the door. There was no way to know if anyone was there – it wasn't Sunday – but they wouldn't know if they didn't try.

No answer.

Now Matthew knocked a bit louder. "Hello," he shouted.

Still nothing.

In desperation, Matthew pounded on the door with his fist. When no one came to the door, he tried the door handle. It was unlocked. As he opened the door, he and Miriam crept slowly inside.

The large room they entered was dark. There were windows all around but they were covered with heavy, canvas drapes. There were benches lined up facing the opposite wall from the door, and a pulpit of sorts at the front.

In order to see, they left the front door slightly ajar and walked forward toward the front of the room. There was an attic entry on the ceiling to the rear of the room and Matthew whispered to Miriam, "Maybe we should see if'n someone's upstairs."

"If'n someone was upstairs, the ladder would be down," she replied.

"Well, you's right, ain't ya?" he said with a nod. She smiled at him. "Maybe out back?" he asked.

There was a door that led to the outside at the rear of the meeting place. Matthew pushed it open and there, several feet from the back steps, was an old woman bent over picking apples off of the ground which had fallen from the tree above her.

Miriam called to her, "Excuse me, Maam." She didn't seem to hear Miriam's call. Nor did she react in any way.

They moved closer to her. As they got just close enough to tap her on the shoulder, she suddenly jumped and looked at them fearfully.

"We's sorry, Maam," Matthew said. "We didn't mean to startle ya none. We's not gonna hurt ya 'r nuthin'. We jus' needs some help."

She looked back and forth at Matthew and Miriam with a confused look on her face. Seeing that they didn't appear to be threatening her, she heaved a deep sigh and then pointed to her ears. Shaking her head she shook her head from side to side.

"She cain't hear us, Matthew," Miriam said. Miriam and Matthew both nodded at the old woman, letting her know they understood.

Miriam began to try to talk with the woman by moving her hands in such a way that the woman might understand. She put her hands together in the typical symbol for prayer, pointed to both herself and Matthew and then put her hand flat at the level of her hips indicating a child. No doubt the woman would think the child was theirs if she understood, but for now, that didn't matter.

The woman seemed to be with her so far. She nodded and repeated the symbol for the child.

Matthew shook his head, "Yes."

Encouraged, Miriam continued. Again, she placed her hand flatly at hip level and then followed it with one hand to her stomach and the other palm open to her forehead. She repeated the movements to be sure the old woman understood.

Suddenly, the old woman's eyes lit up. She reached over to Miriam and put her right hand on Miriam's head and with her left, once again, made the hand signal for a small child.

Matthew and Miriam smiled with relief and said, "Yes" in unison.

The woman looked behind them and then looked up at them questioningly as if to ask where the child was.

"She thinks Winnie is with us," Miriam said to Matthew.

Matthew pointed to the place where they had walked from. Then he waved his hand as if to say that they had come far.

The old woman nodded and with a serious look on her face, as if considering what to do next, she waved them back into the meeting house.

On a piece of paper she began to draw a map. The diagram showed the road they were on and the building they stood inside. She drew an arrow pointing further down the path to the place where a small creek ran across the road. There was apparently a small bridge of some kind that crossed over the creek. Just beyond the bridge she drew a right-hand arrow that pointed into what she showed as trees.

She looked up at them and putting her hands above her head made a symbol for antlers.

"A deer path?" Matthew asked. He repeated her motions to let her know he understood. She drew a very crooked line zigzagging along until it stopped at what appeared in her sketch to be a house.

She pounded her finger onto the place where the house was.

"Okay, thank ya," Miriam said.

The old woman put a hand on each of their arms and then smiling pointed to the door.

Chapter Forty-Five

Back at the camp Henry tried to keep Winnie as cool as possible but nothing seemed to be working. They had cleared a place in the dirt for her to lie down. The earth was cool even on the warmest of days. Henry sat beside her. She used his leg for a pillow. Winnie seemed to be very tired, and it was clear that Gert and Iris were fearful it was some kind of affliction that might be life-threatening. Iris went in search of a pond or spring that might bring them more water to cool the little girl. Gert kept Harriet quiet and spent time preparing food for the small group.

Winnie was very restless. She seemed to be moving in and out of consciousness – moaning while transitioning in between, and Henry was very worried. He gently touched her arm with his fingertips and whispered, "Shhhhhh, Baby Girl," but he had a bad feeling about what might be wrong. He wondered if Miriam and Matthew had found help. He wondered how long they could possibly wait.

After Iris had returned and while Gert, Harriet and Winnie all slept, Iris sat down beside Henry and asked if he'd like a break. "You gots to be gittin" stiff, Henry. I kin hold Winnie. Git yerself somethin' to eat and stretch yerself. If'n she wakes, I'll call to ya," Iris said.

"I could use a good stretch, Iris. Thanks," Henry said, and he slowly moved holding

Winnie's head gently until Iris could slide her leg beneath.

"If'n yous okay here, I's jus' gonna walk a short ways and git some wood for a fire," Henry said. "But you call me if'n Winnie needs me, will ya?"

"Donchu worry none, Henry. We's jus' fine. Maybe I'll close my eyes a little too," Iris said with a smile.

"You do that," Henry replied as he began to walk off.

After he relieved himself behind a tree, Henry took his shirt off and began walking down a path not far from the clearing where everyone was resting. The day was humid and it felt good to be bare-chested for a while. As he walked he picked up a few sticks but it wasn't long before his heart began to feel very sad.

He'd heard from the preacher man back on the plantation before he'd left that he would be able to get from Alabama to Ohio in about a week by wagon.

They'd traveled by boat, wagon and the power of their own feet over the course of so many days now that Henry'd forgotten how long they'd even been on the road, and they still weren't to Ohio. With women and children it would certainly take longer, of course. And they had been fortunate enough to stay with wonderful people who fed, clothed them, and allowed them time to feel safe and rested. He was grateful for all of those things.

However, Henry was suddenly filled with a sense of loss. He wondered how the people back on the plantation were doing. How were Mama and Josiah? Winnie hadn't asked about them for over a week. Was she forgetting already?

Would he?

He knew the outcome would be worth the trip but he began to feel as if it might never end. As the wave of angst washed over him, tears welled up in his eyes. He looked up to the heavens above, closed his eyes, and prayed, "Lord, please help us. I been tryin' to do everythin' I kin to git Winnie north – to git all o' us north – an' the folks I's with is such good people. But, Lord, I's worried for Winnie and for all o' us. Please help us, Lord." Henry knelt on the ground, put his hands over his face and wept.

After about fifteen minutes of tough crying, Henry felt spent. His tears fell in whimpers now. He felt alone but he felt stronger. It was as if he had wept poison out of his own body and now he was more capable of continuing the journey.

He stood up, picked up the sticks he had collected and began to walk back to the camp. Only a few feet down the path he heard Iris calling him. She didn't sound desperate, but she sounded concerned.

He began to run.

Entering the area, he saw that both women and children were awake. Winnie was crying and holding her ears.

"She says her ears is hurtin'," Iris said.

"Maybe she's got some kind o' infection," Gert said.

"What does we do 'bout that?" Henry asked.

"My Mama used to put warm oil in my ears if'n they'd git t' hurtin'," replied Iris.

"Does we got any oil?" Henry asked.

"No, we ain't," Gert answered.

Henry picked Winnie up and held her close. "You's gonna be okay, Winnie," he whispered. She still felt very warm. "We got any more water?" he asked the women.

"Jus' a little," Gert said. "But we cain't give it all to Winnie, Henry. My baby need some too. It's awful hot."

Henry knew she was right. "We's gonna have to go back to that lake. We knows where it is. I'll carry Winnie." And Henry began acting as if they would just pick up and leave right away.

"What 'bout Miriam and Matthew?" Iris asked.

"How'd they know where we'd be? I ain't leavin' my husband, Henry," Gert said powerfully.

"Of course ya ain't," Henry started. "I knows where that lake is. I's gonna take Winnie with me and then I'll come back here afterwards. You stay put. I'll be quick 'bout it." He picked up the empty canteens and swung them over his shoulder.

"Henry," Iris said. "Wouldn't it be faster if'n ya left Winnie here? You could git the water and be back sooner without carryin' her."

Henry considered it for only a moment. "No," he replied. "I gots to take her with me so's I kin dunk her in the water to cool her down."

"But what if Miriam and Matthew bring help and Winnie's not here?" Gert asked.

"It's a chance I's gonna take," Henry said with conviction. "Maybe I'll see 'em on the road. You women take care. I'll be back as quick as I kin." With that, Henry began walking back toward Byrd Lake.

Chapter Forty-Six

Miriam and Matthew had followed the map that the old woman had drawn and were now moving through a wooded area zigzagging back and forth past lilac, butterfly and forsythia bushes. The trees were wild cherry, maple and bald cypress. It was a lovely forest – unassuming and peaceful. Warblers sang their sharp, musical trills and Miriam – though feeling hasty – was enjoying the quiet hike.

Through a clearing they saw the small house that was also shown on the old woman's map. Blueberry bushes encircled the small yard and two friendly dogs barked happily as if welcoming them to the dwelling.

The front door opened and a woman came outside yelling, "Beamer! Rebel! What are y'all barkin' 'bout?" Then she noticed Miriam and Matthew.

The woman appeared to be in her late twenties. She was a small, attractive woman – thinly built. Her hair was tied behind her head in a blond pony-tail and her grey dress bore a white apron with a blue eye-let lace just above the bib and two large pockets.

She put her hand up to shield the sun that shone on her face. "Welcome, strangers. Please feel free to come closer," she offered.

Miriam and Matthew walked toward the woman.

"I's Rachel Cook. My husband, Arnold, is huntin' right now with our sons, Abraham and Wilson." She could see their hesitation, yet there was something else...what was it? Fear? She waved them over to her. "Come closer. It's fine. You're perfectly safe here. Would ya like somethin' to eat or drink?"

Matthew and Miriam quickly looked at one another and then back to Rachel. "Somethin' to drink would be very nice," Matthew answered.

Rachel walked over to a water pump and siphoned fresh water from an underground well and gave them each a ladle of cool water to drink. Once they seemed more comfortable Rachel offered them to go inside the house where they might sit and be out of the direct sunlight.

Walking into the home of this kind woman, Matthew and Miriam were struck by the beautiful quilts that were piled knee-high on the small table in the kitchen. She noticed their interest.

"I does quilting for extra money and sells 'em at the market in Crossville the first Saturday of the month." She looked carefully at them, and asked, "Would ya like to see them?"

Miriam replied quickly, "I sho'ly would, Miss Rachel, but we's here for another reason and I'm afraid time is o' the essence."

"Then let's set down and you tells me what ya needs," she said quite seriously.

Matthew and Miriam sat on Miss Rachel's lovely brown and beige Neo-Rococo style sofa. The cherry wood trim was beautifully crafted and upon sitting down they were both surprised at the soft but firm comfort of it.

Rachel sat on a red and brown striped chair of the same style. "What kin I do for ya?" she asked.

"We's travelin' north to Ohio, and then Canada," Matthew started. "There's seven o' us all together. One is a little girl – jus' under eight years old. Her name's Winnie. Winnie woke up this mornin' burnin' with a fever. We did everythin' we could but it ain't goin' down an' we's worried for her."

Rachel sat forward. "Is there any other symptoms?"

This time Miriam spoke. "No, well, other than she's real sleepy. We tried coolin' her down with water and stripped her clothes but we's not sho' what else we kin do."

"The kindly deaf lady at the church down yonder told us you could help," Matthew added as he handed her the hand-drawn map.

Rachel looked at the map for a moment. "Oh, yes. Mrs. Hews. She's an angel." Looking up at both of them, Rachel put her hand out and touched Miriam's arm. "I kin help ya," she said. "First ya gotta take me to her," Rachel said as she stood up.

She walked over to a closet, opened the door and pulled out a leather bag. "I's a bit o' a doctor," she said. "I learned doctorin' from the injuns. They calls their docs Shaman's," she continued. "I grew up in Kentucky near a Chickasaw tribe," she explained as she looked through her bag and added a few things from a kitchen cupboard. "The Chickasaw's always had roots in nature. Shamanism ain't a religion. It's a practice o' healing. But the practice o' shamanism and many other types o' spiritual healin' involves the belief in a Spirit, or many spirits. Shaman's are like religious doctors," Rachel said. "Let me leave a note for Arnold and the boys." She began writing. "Which way's we headed?"

"We's goin' toward Crossville," Matthew answered.

"Well, that's jus' fine. I'll leave my apron behind," she said as she untied it and slipped it over her head. "Ol' Rebel will be able to pick up on my scent and Arnold and the boys kin help us help y'all." She finished writing the note to her husband and said, "Let's git the wagon and you kin lead the way."

They were very grateful for a ride in the wagon. Rachel had them seated in the back just in case they ran up against someone who might bother them but the road was clear the whole way.

As they neared the place where they'd have to once again walk through the forest, Rachel parked her wagon off the road a good distance and tied the horse to a tree. "How far is it?" she asked.

"Not too far," Matthew said. "'bout twenty minutes or so, I recon."

As they came over a slight grade they saw Henry coming toward them carrying Winnie in his arms. When he saw them, especially with someone who was going to help them, he almost collapsed with relief.

"Henry!" Miriam exclaimed. Turning to Rachel, Miriam said, "This is Winnie."

Rachel laid a light blanket down on the mossy earth beside the path. "Lay her here," she said.

Henry placed the little girl gently on the blanket. Winnie was awake but quite obviously very uncomfortable. "Hi, Winnie," Rachel said to her. "I'm Rachel. I'm a friend o' Matthew and Miriam and I'm going to help ya feel better, okay?"

Winnie nodded – her brows creased to the center of her face. She was obviously uncomfortable.

"Kin ya tell me if anythin' hurts, Winnie?" Rachel asked.

"My ears," Winnie answered, putting her fingers on the outside of the ear canal. "My ears hurts a lot."

"Okay, Winnie. That's jus' what I needed to know," Rachel said as she smiled at the youngster. "Now tell me, does yer tummy or anythin' else hurt ya?"

Winnie shook her head 'no.'

"Alright then, Winnie. I have some things for ya that's gonna fix ya right up, okay?"

"Okay," Winnie answered in a meek voice. She looked at Henry. "Henry, kin ya hold me?"

Henry quickly moved to the little girl and knelt beside her. "I'll always hold ya, Winnie," he said.

Miriam put her hand on Henry's shoulder.

As Rachel pulled a few things out of her little bag, Matthew asked Miriam if it would be okay with them if he went back to the camp to stay with the women.

Rachel looked up at him and said, "Bring 'em back here with ya, Matthew. I's goin' make sho' ya gits to Ohio once Winnie's feelin' better."

Matthew looked at Miriam and Henry and then back to Rachel. "Yes, Maam," he said smiling, and he took off at a quick pace to tell Gert and Iris the good news.

Chapter Forty-Seven

Rachel gave Winnie some water and a mixture she ground together from dried blueberries and goldenseal which is an herb from the buttercup family. This mixture was somewhat sweet and Winnie drank it down eagerly.

"That'll help her ears but we's got to git some hot water to make some Elder Flower tea for her fever," Rachel explained. "Fever's ain't such bad things causin' they burns the sickness away but Elder Flower's help to keep the fever from gittin" too high so it kin do its job without hurtin' Winnie."

Henry and Miriam felt so grateful for having found Rachel.

It was only about an hour later that Iris, Gert, Harriet and Matthew came walking down the path with their supplies in hand.

"How's she doin'?" Iris asked.

"Good," Henry answered.

Miriam introduced Rachel to the rest of their 'family.'

"You folks could probably all do with some soft hay to rest on and a good, hot meal. Once Winnie feels jus' a bit better, we'll move her," she said.

"We don't want t' take advantage, Miss Rachel. You's been so kind already," Miriam said. "But we's real grateful."

"It's my pleasure, Miriam. There ain't no sense in keepin' human bein's as property. It ain't Christian and it ain't moral. I guess I'd do jus' 'bout anythin' I kin to help y'all find yer freedom," Rachel said quite seriously.

They all sat quietly down beside Rachel, Henry and Winnie feeling grateful, exhausted and hopeful for tomorrow.

Chapter Forty-Eight

Several hours later, as Winnie slept, Matthew noticed some movement on the path. Just as he began to feel nervous, he recognized Rachel's hound dog, Rebel sprinting toward them – his tail wagging happily.

Rachel looked up and smiled. "Arnold, Abraham and Wilson must jus' be 'round the bend," she said as she stood up. Sure enough, all three of them rounded the corner in the next few moments. "Mom!" little Wilson exclaimed as he ran to her side. Throwing his arms around her waist, he hugged her. She bent just far enough to kiss his sandy-colored hair. He looked to be about Josiah's age –nearly six. Abraham was just a bit older – maybe ten or eleven and looked very much like his father.

Arnold Cook was a tall man of stalky build. He had a full dark beard and carried a large shotgun in his right hand.

He bent down and kissed Rachel on the cheek then he nodded to the small group of runaways. Rachel introduced everyone and explained the situation to her husband.

He didn't say anything for a minute. He seemed to be thinking about their circumstances. Then he said, "Boys, you help these folks with their belongings. We're going to get everyone home to a nice supper and some rest. Tomorrow we'll plan on how to get everyone safely north."

The boys quickly obeyed their father's instructions. Henry picked Winnie up and held her close.

Rachel smiled at Miriam and then at Matthew. "You heard 'em," she said. "Let's git some supper."

Chapter Forty-Nine

The Cooks had helped many runaways in the past. They'd been part of the early abolitionist movement. The first American abolitionist movement in the United States was transformed by William Lloyd Garrison and reached its peak 1840-1850. The movement had little to do with the actual abolition of slavery, which was a war measure carried out by Abraham Lincoln and the Republican Party in 1862-65. The forces that were lined up for the continuation of slavery were strong and numerous; the abolitionists were few in number and had no political power before 1860 but were guided by a strong religious belief and the moral need to right a horrible wrong.

Mr. Cook had been raised in New England and was about as proper as he could be when it came to the treatment of other human beings. He was a quiet man whose heart was large. It was quite obvious that he loved his wife and sons more than anything in the world.

Once the Cooks had delivered the runaways back to the house, Rachel began cooking dinner while Arnold prepared a bedroom for Winnie and the other ladies in the group.

Winnie was in no way better yet, but she appeared to be far more comfortable and her temperature seemed a bit lower too.

Miriam sat with her while the others washed up and helped Arnold and Rachel with the housework and preparations.

About thirty minutes had passed when Henry came into Winnie's room and saw Miriam dozing in the rocking chair beside the bed. He stood in the doorway for a moment – his heart swelled with love for her. When he'd first felt these feelings it frightened him a bit. In a way he felt as if he was being disloyal to Delia by caring for Miriam. But as the days and weeks had passed, he'd found that his connection with Miriam felt too natural for it be something that was wrong. Besides, he knew that Delia loved him enough that she'd want him to be happy. What they had shared was timeless.

He walked over to Miriam and knelt down in front of her. As he took her hand in his she opened her eyes. When she saw him she smiled.

"Did I drift off?"

"You're worn out," Henry said to her. "Let me take over sittin' with Winnie. I already cleaned up. Go git somethin' ta eat and git some rest." He put his hand on her cheek.

She placed her hand over his and closing her eyes, she seemed to be absorbing his adoration for her. Finally, she sighed and opened her eyes. She glanced over to Winnie.

"She seems to be resting fine," Henry said. "Now, go git some food and rest."

He held her hand as she stood up. "Thank you, Henry," she said as she walked out of the room.

After the door closed, Henry sat on the side of the bed. Winnie stirred. He bent over and kissed her on the cheek.

"We's gonna be jus' fine, Baby Girl," he whispered. "I really think so..."

Just about twenty minutes later Winnie awoke. As soon as she saw Henry she smiled. He hugged her close.

"Where is we, Henry?" she asked looking around the room. "This sho' is a nice bed." She patted her hands on the mattress.

"We's at Miss Rachel and Master Arnold's house, Winnie. They's been real kind ta us and is gonna take us north."

"Oh," Winnie replied. "When's we goin'?"

"Not for another day or two, Winnie. You's been sick. We's gonna be sho' you're well 'fore we travels again," he answered. "You hungry, Baby?" he asked her.

"Yeah, I is," she replied but then added, "Henry, I seen Delia when I was sleepin' an' she tol' me to tell ya somethin'."

Henry knew that Winnie probably had seen Delia. He'd seen and talked to her so many times – he knew it was real. "What'd she say, Winnie?"

"She come to me, and hugged me real close like. She tol' me I was gonna git better real quick and not to worry. Then she asked me if'n I'd tells ya somethin' and when I said I would she got down real close to my face and she said, 'remind him to go through Aberdeen.'"

Chapter Fifty

For the next two days Henry, Winnie, Matthew, Gert, Harriet and Iris lived with the Cook family in their farmhouse. They earned their keep cleaning, cooking, mending and farming. After a couple of days of Rachel Cook's undivided attention and wonderful doctoring skills, Winnie's health improved.

On the third evening Arnold sat in on the beautiful Neo-Rococo style chair with a pipe in his teeth and said to the group, "We're leaving tomorrow. Rachel, I would like you ladies to begin preparation for the trip. We'll need at least a week's worth of rations. Henry, I'd like you and Matthew to help with water and other items that we might need along the way. We have two wagons that we'll travel in. You folks will travel behind us. We'll have to act as if you are our property but we shouldn't have any problems. Generally people don't question these kinds of things when black folks are traveling with whites."

He was very matter-of-fact about it which made everyone feel very much at ease.

"We'll be able to take you as far as Dover in Kentucky. We know people there who can help you the rest of the way. Ripley is only a short distance away by water. There's a gentleman on the other side of the Ohio River named Reverend John Rankin. Our friend will direct you to his home."

Rev. John Rankin was born in Tennessee in 1793. In 1822, after preaching for several years in Kentucky, Rankin and his wife Jean moved his growing family across the Ohio River to Ripley in the free state of Ohio. In 1822, he began his 44 year ministry of Ripley's Presbyterian church. In 1825, he built the house on Liberty Hill overlooking the river.

With its proximity to the river and its owner's fierce opposition to slavery, the Rankin home was a perfect choice to become a stopping point on the Underground Railroad. The Rankin family (which included 13 children) was proud of never having lost a "passenger". Most of the 2,000 escaped slaves who traveled through Ripley stayed with the Rankins.

Henry felt ungrateful bringing up the suggestion to go to Ohio through Aberdeen. It sounded to him as if things were so well planned out he might offend the Cook's kindness by asking to go a different route. Perhaps he would wait until they were in Dover to bring it up.

As the morning sun peeked over the trees the next day, the group of three men, four women and four children set off for northern Kentucky.

Chapter Fifty-One

That first day they traveled over small hills and valleys, through mostly farm and forest land. Just a short time after passing through Jamestown, Tennessee they crossed the border into Kentucky.

Passing through towns named Monticello and Burnside, they crossed a river over a long wooden bridge that swayed with the weight of the wagons.

Just outside of the town of Somerset, Kentucky the group stopped to camp. Rachel had brought plenty of food and they all relaxed around a fire. Arnold told ghost stories that were more funny than frightening. After the children had fallen asleep on a pile of soft blankets, Rachel explained to the adults that they'd be passing through Lexington, Kentucky tomorrow afternoon some time. She explained that there might be some hostile people in and around Lexington.

In the context of the American Civil War, the term "border states" refers to the five slave states of Delaware, Kentucky, Maryland, Missouri and West Virginia which bordered a free state and were aligned with the Union. All but Delaware shared borders with states that joined the Confederacy. In Kentucky and Missouri, there were both pro-Confederate and pro-Union government factions.

Kentucky represented the last slave state before freedom in the North. The state had more than 700 miles of border with Free states, spread over 24 counties—all within a 75-mile radius of some of Kentucky's largest slave-holding centers. In addition, Cincinnati and many surrounding towns to its north and east contained large Quaker and anti-slavery Presbyterian and Methodist communities, as well as some 400 free black residents. Those factors combined to make Kentucky a great pass-through state for Africans escaping to freedom.

"We're headin' toward Dover, Kentucky. But before we gits there, we might run into folks who doesn't want black folks around unless they's in chains. There's talk of skirmishes all over and I cain't say we'll have a clear way through," Rachel said.

"But I thought ya said that long as we was with you, the white folks would think we was yer property and wouldn't bother with us none?"

As Rachel began to start to speak, Arnold put his hand up and replied. "It isn't that they'll bother with us – or you. It's that you might see things that will sicken you. Kentucky is a state where one either wants the slaves freed or one wants the slaves kept down even more than they already are," he said as he looked at each of them. "You might see hardships that are unspeakable."

Henry, Miriam, Matthew, Gert and Iris listened to what was being said but didn't seem much moved by it.

Henry spoke first. "Master Arnold, I knows you an' Miss Rachel's tryin' to prepare us so's we don't give ourselves away none but I's not sho' you knows what we all been through already. I don't 'spect we could see anythin' worse than things we already seen."

The Cooks were both silent for a minute then Arnold spoke again. "I imagine you're right," he said.

"Let's git us some sleep now," Rachel said.

Henry laid awake long after he heard the others softly, slowly breathing into their dreams. He looked up at the stars that peeked through the poplar and emerald ash trees, and closing his eyes he let his thoughts speak to Delia – wherever she might be. "We's almost there," he reflected.

Just then, he saw Delia standing in front of him. *"You take care, Henry. Remember, I's always here with ya."*

Chapter Fifty-Two

When European settlers arrived on the scene, the Kentucky region was in use as a hunting ground for numerous Native American tribes. Daniel Boone was one of the first Anglo-Saxons to explore the area.

Lexington was founded in 1775, seventeen years before Kentucky became a state. William McConnell and a group of frontier explorers were camped at a natural spring when word came from nearby Fort Boonesboro that the first battle of the American Revolution had been fought in Lexington, Massachusetts. In honor of the battle, the group named their site "Lexington". By 1820, Lexington, Kentucky, was one of the largest and wealthiest towns west of the Allegheny Mountains.

Planters held slaves for use as artisans and laborers, field hands and domestic servants. In the city, slaves worked primarily as domestic servants and artisans, although they also worked with merchants, shippers and a wide variety of trades. In 1850, one fifth of the state's population were slaves, and Lexington had the highest concentration of slaves in the state.

As a slaveholding state with a considerable abolitionist population, Kentucky was eventually caught in the middle during the Civil War, supplying both Union and Confederate forces with thousands of troops.

As the Cook's two wagons traveled down the main streets of Lexington, they passed bustling businesses, beautiful mansions and traffic heavier than they'd ever seen. There were wonderful smells of coffee and bakery items and the sound of music from saloons all in the same block.

Winnie was especially fascinated by the intriguing sights and sounds, and asked Henry if they could stop to look inside the lovely Christ Episcopal Church. Rachel explained, however, that they wouldn't be allowed in the church because they were black. Rachel also explained that there were colored churches in and around Lexington too but it might be best to just keep moving. She told them that they'd be in Ripley, Ohio by tomorrow if they could make it as far as Millersburg by this evening. They all agreed that getting to Ohio was the most important thing for now.

As they traveled just outside Lexington, leaving the sounds and smells of the city behind them, and rode closer to the small town of Hutchison they began to hear gunfire.

Arnold stopped. Listening for the direction of the shooting and trying to assess what was causing it, he quickly realized that the sound was coming from slave catchers.

"Stay close," he yelled back at Henry who was driving the second wagon. "No matter what you see or hear, just keep following my wagon."

Only five minutes later, in the distance Arnold and Henry could see a woman and her two young children running quickly through the field ahead of them. She was running toward them. Arnold knew that he could not allow them to climb into the wagons. Doing that would threaten everyone else.

As she got a little closer, the sight of three men on horses firing their guns into the air could be seen. They kicked the sides of their mounts, and picking up speed began to close in on the poor woman and her little ones.

"Help me!" she screamed. But no sooner were the words of her mouth than the butt of one of the rider's guns hit her in the head and she fell to the ground with a thud.

Henry and Matthew could barely stand to watch. Miriam held Winnie close and covered her eyes from the sight.

The children who had so bravely run with their mother now wailed, laying themselves over their mother's still body.

The three men dismounted and heaved the bleeding, unconscious woman onto one of the horses. Then the children were placed each on the other two horses and as they rode away one of them men could be heard screaming at the children to "shut up" and threatening that the same thing would happen to them if they weren't quiet.

The only sound anyone heard as they galloped away was the sound of the horse's hooves and the wheels of the Cook's wagons as they continued northeast toward Ripley.

Chapter Fifty-Three

That night, as they camped just outside of Millersburg, each of them was lost in their own quiet thoughts and feelings. At one point, after the others were asleep, Miriam asked Henry if they could take a short stroll and talk a little.

Walking a short distance away from the rest of the group, Miriam spoke first. "Henry, what we seen today was..." She paused, unable to describe her feelings. She had been through so much: between her husband being sold away and the unanswered questions surrounding the loss of her son, Aaron, her heart was wounded to her core. But her whole life experience – being enslaved, abused and exploited as well as watching so many others tortured and even killed – these things had taken their toll on her very deeply.

She covered her hands over her eyes and began to weep. Henry pulled her close. He didn't say anything at first. He, too, felt a lump of sorrow swell in his throat. He'd seen a lot of horrendous things, but never had he seen the desperation or brutality that he'd seen today. How would he ever be able to help Miriam or Winnie forget that horrific scene?

As Miriam wept, Henry stroked her head gently. "We's gonna git out o' here, Miriam. You, me and Winnie," he said. "We's goin' as far north as ya wants to. We kin go to Canada if'n ya wants. I'll make sure ya gits there, Miriam."

Miriam looked up at him. He wiped the tears off of her face.

"I cares 'bout ya so much," Henry began. "We's been through a lot together since we met. I ain't never known a stronger woman who's so kind too." Henry paused a moment looking deeply into Miriam's eyes. "I never thought I'd say this to anyone again, Miriam, but – as soon as we's free - I'd be proud if'n you'd consider bein' my wife."

Her eyes widened. "Henry..." she replied in a surprised tone. "You knows how I feels 'bout ya. I loved my poor husband too but I ain't never known anyone like you neither. You makes me feel safe. Still, Henry, it's a big decision - ya sho' 'bout this?"

Henry bent his head toward her and kissed her mouth softly. "I loves ya, Miriam. You, me and Winnie – we'd be a family. We could have kids of our own too. I'm so proud to know ya – to have shared all this with ya," he said. And smiling, he said, "We makes a good team, you and me."

"We does, Henry," she said, suddenly feeling hopeful and happy for the first time since they had witnessed the poor woman and her children being abused by the slave catchers.

"Yes, I'll marry ya," she replied.

Chapter Fifty-Four

The next morning Arnold awoke everyone just before the sun rose over the meadow. "It's going to be a long, tiring day," he said. "We need to find a man in Dover who'll help ya cross the Ohio River into Ripley. We can make it but it'll easily take all day and part of the night. The road goes through farmland and over hills that are sometimes very rough." He paused. "I don't need to warn ya that we may also come across more slave catchers."

Each of them looked at one another. Henry put his hand on Miriam's. "We'll be fine, Master Arnold," he said.

Feeling the tension and anticipation of their day ahead, Rachel said, "Okay, then – let's git breakfast together so we kin git goin'."

It wasn't long before the small party was on the road again. They traveled past large farms that lined the dirt path moving northeast from Millersburg toward Dover. About eight hours into their travels, just outside of the town of Sardis, the small hills of northern Kentucky came into view. The White and Chestnut Oak tree's leaves blew happily in the late afternoon breeze above the mountain bogs, cliffs, and rock overhangs that they passed. There were beautiful Shortleaf and Virginia Pine as well as Sugarberry, Green Ash, Pecan, and American Elm along the way. Miriam said that it was "beautiful country," and Gert said that she hoped their new home was as "lovely as these woods." They were all impressed with the splendor of the hills and valleys that they traversed through.

Still, the day was wearing on and they were all getting tired. Arnold suggested that instead of trying to make it all the way through as they had originally planned, they camp overnight in the hills just east of Old Washington and then finish the last ten to twelve miles in the morning. Everyone agreed knowing that tomorrow was going to be a very big day. They camped near a small spring beside Hydrangea, Honeysuckle and Juniper bushes. The fragrance was heavenly and after a supper of beans and dried pork, Rachel suggested they say a prayer of Thanksgiving for the miles they'd left behind them and to ask for good fortune for the trip ahead.

Taking each other's hands, they bowed their heads and Arnold prayed, "Dear Lord, we stand together today, your servants in Christ, to thank you for bringing us this far and holding us so safely in your arms. Also, heavenly Father, we pray for your continued love..." Before Arnold could finish the prayer, gunfire sprayed through the forest.

Henry, Matthew and Arnold crouched down atop the children and the ladies dove for the ground.

"Douse the fire," Iris whispered, and Matthew threw a blanket over the low flames.

They heard hoof beats, dogs barking, and people screaming but they didn't seem to be coming toward their location. Instead, they were moving quickly away.

After waiting a few tense moments, Arnold told everyone the threat was gone. Winnie ran to Henry and held him close.

"Don't chu worry, Baby Girl. I ain't lettin' nuthin' harm ya," he said as he kissed her head.

"Maybe we ought to git some sleep. We's got a big day ahead o' us tomorra," Rachel said.

They each laid their heads down that night knowing it would be their last night sleeping as slaves.

Chapter Fifty-Five

The next morning was overcast. Nothing, however, could have kept the mood of the day at bay. It was filled with feelings of excitement as the small party packed one last time and headed north toward Dover. On occasion a few drops of rain fell from the sky but most of the day was dry and overcast.

They traveled past Germantown to the west and then through the small town of Minerva just about five miles south of Dover. It wasn't an easy ride – the roads were dirt and stone and they were always on the lookout for slave catchers but it would have taken a lot more than a little apprehension to darken their day.

Just before noon they arrived in Dover and went directly to the home of David McHennesy. David was an old man who lived in a small house on the edge of town. He'd known Arnold's father years ago and the two had stayed in touch even after Arnold's father had passed away. Mr. McHennesy was a sworn abolitionist and wasn't afraid to admit it. He was older but he had a lot of life in him.

Dover, Kentucky sits right on the edge of the Ohio River just upstream from Ripley, Ohio on the other side. The town was small but the people in the town were typically abolitionists. Dover was a very busy Underground Railroad stop and most of the people in the town were well organized and able to move runaways before slave catchers even knew they had arrived in town.

Mr. McHennesy was good friends with the man who ran the ferry boat that took folks from one side of the river to the other. That same ferry boat would take the seven escapees to the shores of Ripley where they could climb the long set of stairs to the John Rankin home and find a safe haven.

In Ripley, Rankin served as a "conductor" on the Underground Railroad and opened his home to African Americans seeking freedom. His home stood on a three hundred-foot high hill that overlooked the Ohio River. Rankin would signal runaway slaves in Kentucky with a lantern, letting them know when it was safe for them to cross the river. He kept the runaways hidden until it was safe for them to travel further north. Because the United States Constitution and the Fugitive Slave Law of 1850 permitted slave owners to reclaim their runaway slaves, even if the African Americans resided in a free state like Ohio, to truly gain their freedom runaways had to leave the United States. Underground Railroad stops provided runaway slaves with safe houses all of the way to Canada.

"We'll head down river jus' after sunset," David said. "In the meantime, you should hide in the barn behind my house. I'll bring ya somethin' ta eat shortly."

The day seemed to drag by, but as Henry watched Miriam and Winnie nap together, he felt an enormous amount of gratitude and love. Tears stung his eyes as he began to realize that his dream was coming true. Tomorrow they'd awaken in Ohio – a safer haven – and then Reverend Rankin would help them get to Canada and a new life.

Just after supper the Cooks prepared to leave and say good-bye to everyone. Henry felt especially grateful to Rachel for healing Winnie's ear pain and as he kissed Rachel on the cheek, a tear slid down his own. "We wouldn't have been okay without ya, Miss Rachel. I owes ya fer the rest o' my life."

"You don't owe me nuthin', Henry," she told him. "You jus' git these lovely people to Canada and I'll sleep well knowin' I had the chance ta git ta know ya."

They shook Arnold's hand and hugged each of the boys. Before too long, the Cook's wagons were out of sight. There was a mixed feeling of gratitude, sadness and real excitement as the whole group readied itself for their trip across the Ohio.

David McHennesy explained that they would travel down Market Street at dusk. Market Street led directly to the river. He had coordinated with his friend, Samuel, to arrive to the shoreline just about that time. Once the runaways were aboard, the ferry would immediately cross the river to the opposite shore and travel as close to the shoreline as possible until it reached Ripley. Once they docked at Ripley, Samuel would tell them where to hide until they saw Reverend Rankin's lantern. At that point, it would be a climb up the one hundred steps to the safe haven of the Rankin House. Samuel would not be going with them. There was much less risk to them if the ferry boat wasn't docked in any one place for any length of time.

Just after the sun slipped softly over the horizon, the small group walked down to the river. Waiting near the water and under the cover of trees they finally saw the small ferry boat chugging down the Ohio.

Miriam looked at Henry and she saw him mouth the words, "I love ya." She smiled and holding Winnie close, felt a sudden rush of happiness as she realized that her life with Henry was just around the corner.

Chapter Fifty-Six

There was barely time to thank Mr. McHennesy as Samuel rushed the runaways on board. "We's gotta git goin'," he said. "They's some slave runners jus' up the river a mile 'r so. We kin beat 'em but we cain't take too much time."

"Is we gonna be okay?" Gert asked.

"We'll be fine," Matthew answered her. "We didn't come this far to end up back in chains."

"Let's jus' git goin'," Samuel said.

And without more than a wave goodbye to Mr. McHennesy, the small boat pulled away from shore and slowly moved across the wide river to the Ohio side. As the sky got darker, Henry wished that it wasn't such a clear night. The idea of the slave catchers being such a short distance up the river bothered him a little. His thoughts were cut short, however, by the look of concern on Winnie's face.

He bent down and held her hands in his. "What's wrong Baby Girl? You look worried."

She paused for a minute. "Where's we goin', Henry?" She almost looked as if she were going to cry.

"Well, we's goin' to Ripley, Winnie. There's a nice man there who's gonna help us git to Canada and then we'll be free." Henry said this

238

with a smile on his face but Winnie still looked worried.

"We cain't go to Ripley, Henry," she sobbed and leaned into Henry as she began to weep.

He held her close. "Why not, Baby Girl? Reverend Rankin's gonna help us," he said as he stroked her head trying to soothe her.

"Henry," she said, looking up at him with big tears in her eyes. She looked so sad his heart felt like breaking.

"Baby, what is it?" he asked. At this point, Miriam was kneeling down too. Her hand rubbed softly on Winnie's back.

"Henry," Winnie sobbed, "We cain't go through Ripley. We has to go through Aberdeen, remember? She tol' us – go through Aberdeen."

Henry had forgotten Delia's warning. He thought about it for a moment, and then explained to Winnie that Delia was just trying to help them get across to Ohio faster. They *would* have gotten to Ohio faster if they'd gone through Aberdeen – that part was true – but Master Arnold had known that they could more safely cross the river in Dover and that's they way they went.

"Winnie," Miriam said, "everythin' is fine. Henry's right. Delia was jus' tellin' us the shorter way but she didn't know 'bout Mr. McHennesy or Samuel. It's fine."

"We should go through Aberdeen," Winnie said as she softly cried in Henry's arms.

"It's fine, Baby Girl. I ain't lettin' nuthin' hurt ya," he said.

Miriam gave him a concerned look but she knew he was telling the truth. He'd never let any harm come to either one of them.

Chapter Fifty-Seven

The ferry glided slowly through the water toward Ripley. All of them stood on the bow of the boat trying to imagine what it would be like to step foot in Ohio, finally.

Before the American Civil War, a large number of runaway slaves passed through Ohio. Not all runaway slaves chose to remain in Ohio, however. Although slavery was illegal in Ohio, a number of people still opposed the ending of slavery. Many of these people also were opposed to the Underground Railroad. Some people attacked conductors on the Underground Railroad or returned runaway slaves to their owners in hopes of collecting rewards. To truly win their freedom, runaway slaves had to flee all of the way to Canada.

Everyone in the small group realized that the trip was not over once they arrived in Ohio. But they were also aware that the further north they were, the more abolitionists there would be and the safer they would become. In their minds, Ohio was a doorway to freedom.

As they neared the shore just below the town of Ripley, the ferry slowed down and began docking. High above the river there was a light shining far above the ground on a flagpole. They knew this was a sign from Reverend Rankin that it was safe to come to his house. Samuel had told them that once they got to shore they needed to climb the stairs quickly so the slave runners didn't have any chance to see them. It was a clear evening and there were, after all, one hundred steps to climb.

As the boat docked, Henry and Matthew jumped off and temporarily tied the boat to the small pier and then began helping the women and children to shore. Samuel handed them their belongings. Just as they were untying the mooring lines they heard gunshots.

"Git outa here!" screamed Samuel and he ran back to the helm of his boat and steered away from the shore.

Matthew and Henry helped the children and women begin the long trek up the staircase to the Rankin house. Gert carried Harriet and Miriam followed closely behind holding Winnie's hand. Iris went up next followed by Matthew. By the time Henry got onto the steps they could hear the slave runner's boat getting very, very close.

"Hurry," he called ahead. Everyone scrambled as quickly as they could up the long set of stairs.

"Stop, niggers or I'll shoot ya," one of the men called out.

It didn't take long before it sounded like they had made it to shore. There was an enormous sense of danger and urgency as the runaways moved as quickly as they could.

"Stop!" the man screamed and they heard a shot ring out through the evening air.

Everyone was running as fast as they could. They could hear the sound of the slave catcher's feet upon the stairs behind them. Another shot rang out and they heard a thud.

Matthew, who was a bit further up the stairs than Henry, looked behind him. Seeing the men coming very quickly, he screamed at the women to run faster.

At that moment more shots rang out but this time from the landing above them. At the top of the stairs there were two men with shotguns. One of them called out, "Don't ya come no closer, 'r you'll be the one gittin' shot."

The sounds of the slave catcher's feet were silenced. They were no longer perusing the runaways.

Gert and Harriet arrived at the top step. Following quickly behind them was Miriam, Winnie, Iris and then Matthew. Mrs. Rankin tried to herd them to the house as quickly as possible but Matthew and Miriam couldn't see Henry.

"Matthew, where's Henry?" Miriam asked frantically. She remembered having heard the shot and the thud. "Oh, God, no!" she exclaimed and began running back toward the stairs. Winnie screamed.

Matthew caught up with Miriam and told her to take care of Winnie. He'd find Henry. "He prob'ly jus' jumped off the stairs to avoid gittin" hit," he told her. But he knew that Henry'd never leave them open to gunfire. Listening to be sure the sound of the slave catcher's boat was moving away from the dock, Matthew's gut felt twisted as he and the two gentlemen from the Rankin house slowly moved down the staircase in the dark.

About one third of the way down, Matthew – who was first down the steps – saw the shadowy figure of a man slumped on the steps. He moved quickly to Henry's side. 'Thank heavens he didn't roll down the steps!' he thought to himself.

"Henry," Matthew said as he moved to the step below where Henry laid. There was no response. "Henry," he said again as he shook Henry's shoulder.

At that point, the other two gentlemen arrived to the place where Henry was laying.

"How is he?" Reverend Rankin asked.

"He ain't talkin'," Matthew said with tears in his eyes.

"Let me see," Reverend Rankin said as he moved closer to Henry.

Feeling Henry's wrist and neck, Reverend Rankin seemed to be struggling to notice anything that told him that Henry was going to be okay. The other gentleman with Reverend Rankin (whom they later found out was his eldest son, Edward) said, "There's a lot o' blood on the step."

Picking up Henry's head, Reverend Rankin's hand quickly became soaked with blood. He put it down gently. He put his ear down close to Henry's mouth hoping to hear air passing by – even a little. Sitting up, he put his hand on Henry's chest, looked at Matthew and sadly said, "I'm afraid he's gone."

"NO!" Matthew screamed. "He cain't be! Henry! Henry..." and he began to cry.

From atop the hill they heard Miriam screaming. She had heard Matthew's shout of grief. Winnie knew that something was wrong and began to cry. Miriam held her close, crying with her.

Within a few minutes the Rankin's and Matthew carried Henry's lifeless body up the stairs and placed it on the warm grass. Everyone sobbed bitterly as they realized that Henry had taken the bullets instead of them. He had made sure they had gotten to safety. He had helped to guarantee their freedom.

Chapter Fifty-Eight

"Henry," Delia said, *"I's right here – jus' like always."*

Henry stood in front of her, looking into her eyes. There was a blue mist at his feet and the light around them was translucent. Crystalline dewdrops seemed to cling to the invisible space between them, and the sound of a distant melody softly breathed into his Soul.

"Delia!" he said with some surprise in his voice. *"Where is we?"*

"We's where freedom always is, Henry. We's where love always is too," she replied.

"Is I dead, Delia?"

She smiled and took his hands in hers. *"No, Henry, you's more alive than you've ever known before."*

He could feel the warmth of her hands in his. Her skin was soft. Her eyes glowed with a love so deep that he knew it's all she was.

"But what 'bout Winnie, Delia?" he asked. *"What happened? I don't remember nuthin' but runnin' up a hill – tryin' to git away..."*

"Winnie's jus' fine, Henry. Miriam's takin' good care o' her. They's goin' ta make it to Canada. Ya did real good, Henry," she replied with an angel's smile on her face.

"Miriam..." Henry said. *"I loves her, Delia."*

"She loves ya too, Henry. And when there's love between two people – even if they cain't be together – they's always together. She's sad right now but she'll be jus' fine," Delia told him.

Henry looked at Delia. She was beautiful. Everything about her was beautiful. And he had a sense that everything really was going to be just fine.

Epilogue

I've often wondered what it would have been like to live in those times when men and women felt the need to own and control others in such a heartless fashion. I've wondered how they could justify their opinions on humanity.

In many ways I still see these same judgments today: black against white, white against black; American's are afraid of Muslim's; Muslim extremists are critical of American's way of life. There are Native Americans and Eskimo's who are completely ignored by society. There is distaste for Hispanics and daily mockery of Asians. Roman Catholics and Protestants battle for a place in heaven while Israelis and Palestinians battle for a homeland they don't believe they are meant to share. And there is still slavery in the world.

My gut tells me that we live this life for one reason – to learn to love unconditionally – to put aside our opinions, our habitual responses and to move beyond our human experiences. We are here to Love one another.

I believe that on a very infinite level – we already do.

After a proper burial the following day, Reverend Rankin, his lovely wife Jean and their thirteen noble children helped each of the runaways deal with their grief in the most personal ways possible. Everyone's main concern, of course, was Winnie and Miriam. Still, this was a family now; people who'd shared experiences and feelings that would bond them forever. The whole Rankin family was very sensitive to their needs.

The runaways stayed with the Rankin's for a little over two weeks. They were provided new clothes, shoes and some money. As soon as they were able, the newly freed slaves were led by a host of abolitionists to the Canadian border by way of Toledo, Ohio and Detroit, Michigan. They entered Canada two and a half weeks after Henry passed away and eventually settled in Kitchener, Ontario with the help of abolitionist families in Canada.

Matt, Gert and Harriet eventually bought a small house in Waterloo. Matt worked in a cigar shop and eventually opened his own store. They had three more children: Sarah, Christen and their youngest, Henry.

Iris worked in a ladies specialty shop where she eventually married a delivery truck driver and moved to Hamilton. They had two boys: Henry and Matthew.

Miriam and Winnie rented a little flat on the east side of Kitchener and lived there until Winnie eventually got married to a young man who worked in a factory in Guelph. They eventually had three children: Henry, Delia and Josiah. She never saw her mother or brother again but always felt their presence in her heart.

Miriam worked as a seamstress and stayed in the flat in Kitchener until she passed away at the age of seventy-two of a heart condition. She never married after arriving in Canada. She always felt a deep connection to Henry – and somehow – to Delia too. She visited her extended family many times.

Each of them felt a deep gratitude every day for the freedom they were living. They never took for granted the wonderful gifts of being responsible for their own lives. They never forgot the people who sacrificed so much to help them obtain this exquisite thing that most don't even acknowledge that they own: Freedom. Freedom to work – to own property – to buy – to sell – to have families – to come and go as they please; Freedom to act and live as they choose – Freedom to Love.

The Trickle of Time

Moments expire in the trickle of time,
like the breath of the morning and its obvious
rhyme
in the sunset and colors that fade with the night
but return with the sunrise when the morning
takes flight.

It is True that we all can remember the times
in our life that provide such incredible rhymes,
like the raindrops that spill very softly in Spring
and the flowers that bloom with the life that they
bring.

In these moments in time there are moments within
where our Hearts find the Truth and an ember
begins
to embark on new memories that the trickle of time
will forever enliven and within us will shine.

It is here in these moments when I stand in a place
that's aware of your eyes and your touch and your
face
that I find myself grateful that the trickle of time
doesn't wash away moments when your Heart
spoke to mine.

-Anne Jobes

The Emancipation Proclamation
January 1, 1863

A Transcription

By the President of the United States of America:

A Proclamation.

Whereas, on the twenty-second day of September, in the year of our Lord one thousand eight hundred and sixty-two, a proclamation was issued by the President of the United States, containing, among other things, the following, to wit:

"That on the first day of January, in the year of our Lord one thousand eight hundred and sixty-three, all persons held as slaves within any State or designated part of a State, the people whereof shall then be in rebellion against the United States, shall be then, thenceforward, and forever free; and the Executive Government of the United States, including the military and naval authority thereof, will recognize and maintain the freedom of such persons, and will do no act or acts to repress such persons, or any of them, in any efforts they may make for their actual freedom.

"That the Executive will, on the first day of January aforesaid, by proclamation, designate the States and parts of States, if any, in which the people thereof, respectively, shall then be in rebellion against the United States; and the fact that any State, or the people thereof, shall on that day be, in good faith, represented in the Congress of the United States by members chosen thereto at elections wherein a majority of the qualified voters of such State shall have participated, shall, in the absence of strong countervailing testimony, be deemed conclusive evidence that such State, and the people thereof, are not then in rebellion against the United States."

Now, therefore I, Abraham Lincoln, President of the United States, by virtue of the power in me vested as Commander-in-Chief, of the Army and Navy of the United States in time of actual armed rebellion against the authority and government of the United States, and as a fit and necessary war measure for suppressing said rebellion, do, on this first day of January, in the year of our Lord one thousand eight hundred and sixty-three, and in accordance with my purpose so to do publicly proclaimed for the full period of one hundred days, from the day first above mentioned, order and designate as the States and parts of States wherein the people thereof respectively, are this day in rebellion against the United States, the following, to wit:

Arkansas, Texas, Louisiana, (except the Parishes of St. Bernard, Plaquemines, Jefferson, St. John, St. Charles, St. James Ascension, Assumption, Terrebonne, Lafourche, St. Mary, St. Martin, and Orleans, including the City of New Orleans) Mississippi, Alabama, Florida, Georgia, South Carolina, North Carolina, and Virginia, (except the forty-eight counties designated as West Virginia, and also the counties of Berkley, Accomac, Northampton, Elizabeth City, York, Princess Ann, and Norfolk, including the cities of Norfolk and Portsmouth[)], and which excepted parts, are for the present, left precisely as if this proclamation were not issued.

And by virtue of the power, and for the purpose aforesaid, I do order and declare that all persons held as slaves within said designated States, and parts of States, are, and henceforward shall be free; and that the Executive government of the United States, including the military and naval authorities thereof, will recognize and maintain the freedom of said persons.

And I hereby enjoin upon the people so declared to be free to abstain from all violence, unless in necessary self-defence; and I recommend to them that, in all cases when allowed, they labor faithfully for reasonable wages.

And I further declare and make known, that such persons of suitable condition, will be received into the armed service of the United States to garrison forts, positions, stations, and other places, and to man vessels of all sorts in said service.

And upon this act, sincerely believed to be an act of justice, warranted by the Constitution, upon military necessity, I invoke the considerate judgment of mankind, and the gracious favor of Almighty God.

In witness whereof, I have hereunto set my hand and caused the seal of the United States to be affixed.

Done at the City of Washington, this first day of January, in the year of our Lord one thousand eight hundred and sixty three, and of the Independence of the United States of America the eighty-seventh.

By the President: ABRAHAM LINCOLN
WILLIAM H. SEWARD, Secretary of State.

Coming Soon:

Sheena

I live in Stockton, California. Stockton has the impressive honor of being rated the number one most miserable city in the United States by Forbes.com. According to them, only 15% of Stockton adults have a college degree, which is one of the lowest rates in the U.S. Unemployment hit 15% in 2010, while housing prices should keep falling back to their mid-1990s level when the median home price was $130,000.

I actually grew up in Byron, a small town outside of Stockton. My mother is a waitress at the Discovery Bay Country Club. My father works at the small Byron Airport as a custodian. My mother and father are not married but have lived together on and off throughout my whole life.

I was an accident. My mother became pregnant with me when she was still in high school and so she never graduated. My father was working at McDonalds serving up hamburgers and fries. I still don't know why they didn't give me up for adoption (or worse) but I'm here and I have learned to take one day at a time. I don't confuse hope with possibility.

I am nineteen years old and I have been on my own most of my life. Mom and Dad have moved up in the world but, even so, I've never had much of a shot at normalcy. I followed in my mother's footsteps and got pregnant when I was fifteen. I was smart, though. I gave my son up for adoption to a nice couple from Massachusetts who had lots of money and would treat him well. My boyfriend ran so fast when he found out about Jason (that's what I called my son when he was born) that there were no thoughts about keeping the child. Besides I knew what it was like to grow up knowing you were a mistake. My parents never stopped reminding me.

Currently, I live in a small apartment that sits above a bar on East Clay Street on the South Side of Stockton. The area's not all that great but the apartment is cheap and I'm trying to stay independent as long as I can. You see, I'm a prostitute by trade, and what I don't want to do is get myself hooked up with some nasty pimp that's going to beat my ass and take my money. So if I have to live in a mangy, one-room apartment with noisy neighbors and cockroaches, then I will.

I haven't spoken to my parents for months now. They never had time for me anyway. I was always underfoot as far as they were concerned; an expense they couldn't afford. I suspect they were glad to be rid of me when I left after Jason was born.

So, here I am – waking up at two o'clock in the afternoon on a pull-down bed with a nasty mattress hoping there'll be at least a little hot water in the bathroom I share with an old alcoholic named George who gets the D.T.'s[1] and screams at his own invisible demons when he hasn't had enough to drink.

I don't mind old George, though. He really is a nice guy. Sometimes, when he isn't talking crazy or mumbling to himself, I pretend that he is my Grandpa. I never knew any of my grandparents and it's fun to think I have family living so close. Besides, he seems to like me. I actually enjoy doing little things for him that might make his day a bit easier. He is nearly eighty years old and as far as I know he doesn't have any family he keeps in touch with either.

As I pass by his apartment, I hear him rustling around in there so I assume he is okay. "Hello, George," I say as I walk by.

"Humpf," he replied back to me. I smile. George is just fine.

Going into the stained bathroom with my towel, washrag and bathing essentials carried safely in a plastic bag, I turn on the light and am immediately greeted by a big rat that scurries

---

[1] Delirium tremens is a severe form of alcohol withdrawal that involves sudden and severe mental or neurological changes. -**American Accreditation HealthCare Commission**

quickly into a hole in the wall. The rats used to scare me. I don't even jump any longer. I'm used to the rats. I'm used to the cockroaches and the water bugs too. I don't like 'em much and, obviously, they don't like me much either.

The bathroom is small. This is an old building. The white tile on the walls is cracked and discolored with age. The enamel on the tub has been scrubbed so many times (or not) that there's no polish left on the tainted bathtub that probably once shone bright white. The toilet is the worst. No matter how hard I try to make the bathroom somewhat presentable, the toilet still smells. It's stained with rust and brown splatter.

The floor of the bathroom is marked with dirt that has been ground into the pores of the broken tile. I always wear flip-flops into the bathroom and while I shower. I ain't steppin' on all that filth! UGH! I wish I could afford more cleaning supplies.

While I undress, I glance into the broken mirror that hangs above a stopped up sink. Sometimes I wonder if I still look only nineteen or if my lifestyle has made me look older.

I don't smoke or drink. I don't do drugs. Then again, I don't eat right either. And my way of life probably isn't the healthiest way of living. Still, I use condoms and because I work for myself, I am as careful as I can be about who

I screw. I've only been beaten up once and, in my profession, that's pretty good.

As I step into the shower, my thoughts go to the John I had late last evening. He seemed like such a nice fellow. I don't get involved with any of the men who hire me. I don't ask them personal questions. I don't tell them anything about me. I always insist on a cheap hotel room. I don't bring them home. I'm sure I could make more money if I would screw them behind a building or give them head in their cars but I'm not stupid. I'd rather have less money and stay safe.

But that guy last night – he was sorta sweet. His brown shaggy hair fell into his eyes like he hadn't been able to get a hair cut for a long time. At the same time, it looked right on him. His green eyes were clear and he was one of those people who you thought you could get used to having around. He seemed a little shy at first, but once I started touching him, he got so riled up that he screwed me with a passion I hadn't felt for a long time. Most of the guys I'm with just want to get it on, and once they get off they're never interested in *my* pleasure at all.

Now, I'm not usually interested in pleasure with my John's either. It's a business. I do what I do and then I'm done.

But that guy last night – man, he was really good. I pleasured him and then he pleasured me right back. I didn't think I could cum with a John – I never really have – but he brought out a desire I haven't felt for years.

When he handed me my money and an extra $20 I liked him even more. That extra $20 gave me just enough to cover the rent this month with a couple bucks over for a treat. After my shower, I've decided to treat myself to a Big Mac.

The water isn't hot. It is luke-warm. But at least it isn't cold. I'm pretty sure the landlord hasn't purchased a new hot water heater since 1920.

I don't use soap. I use shampoo for everything. I wash my hair first and then before I rinse it out I use the lather to wash my body. It's cheaper that way and it works pretty well. The shower is fast. I hate luke-warm water.

I throw on a short, hot pink skirt, a white tank top that barely covers my breasts and a pair of knee-high, patent leather boots with three-inch heels. I don't know what it is about boots, but the men love them. Whatever! Just so it gets me some business I don't really care any more what it is I have to wear.

Walking down the hall to my room I decide to knock on George's door. He doesn't reply right away, so I knock a second time, calling his name as I do, "Hey, George. It's Sheena."

I hear him grumble again. The door opens a little and the smell of B.O. and alcohol on hot air thrusts itself over me. UGH!

"Hey, George. I'm goin' down to McDonalds in a couple minutes. You want me to bring you back some French fries?" (George loves McDonald's French fries). His eyes light up. I smile. "I'll bring you a large, okay?" He nods and says, "How soon you gonna be back?" "Soon," I say, and he closes the door.

I take my plastic bag back to my room. I hang my towel up over a wooden chair near my little TV table and put my dirty clothes in a laundry basket in the corner. The other things hang off of a door knob.

I have a small, foggy looking mirror on the wall. I apply some make-up and run the comb through my hair again. Fortunately, I've got really good hair. It'll dry with a nice wave and it's just below my shoulders so it's pretty sexy – even if I do say so myself. They guys really like it.

I don't carry anything of importance with me when I go out. I've been robbed only once, but if it happens again I'm not losing all my money or ID again.

I grab my $9.00 in cash, six condoms (hoping for a good night) and the key to my apartment.

I lock the door behind me and head to McDonalds.

Read Anne's other books:

Powerless — Healing From the Addiction of a
Loved One

Love is What's Left

Sheena

Spirits of the Heart - Volume One

Spirits of the Heart - Volume Two

Spirits of the Heart - Volume Three

Of Light and Sound

Journey of the Heart - Volume One

Journey of the Heart - Volume Two

Melancholy Moments

Misunderstood

References

- nyhistory.org

- library.gsu.edu

- wikopedia.com

- http://library.thinkquest.org/J011
  2391/slavery.htm

- http://www.pbs.org/wgbh/aia/par
  t4/4i2977.html

- The History Channel – The
  Underground Railroad

- http://www.ripleyohio.net/htm/ra
  nkin.htm

- The National Archives and
  Records Administration

Made in United States
North Haven, CT
02 July 2024